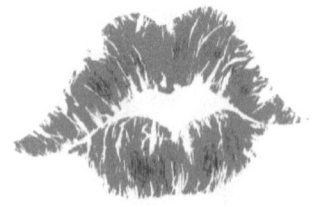

EVERNIGHT PUBLISHING ®

www.evernightpublishing.com

SAM CRESCENT

Copyright© 2022

Sam Crescent

Editor: Karyn White

Cover Art: Sour Cherry Designs

Jacket Design: Jay Aheer

ISBN: 978-1-77339-204-2

NEED

NEED

Trojans MC, 4

Sam Crescent

Copyright © 2015

Chapter One

Crazy watched his daughter, Strawberry, as she played in the park with the other kids. Without his ex-wife around his neck, things at home had become a hell of a lot easier. Suz, his ex, had been a club whore who'd trapped him into a marriage for the sake of his daughter, and Strawberry was his. He'd done the paternity test to confirm that. Running fingers through his hair, he watched his little girl play, sliding down the swings, and generally enjoying life. When he had a chance to reflect, like he did now, he couldn't believe what a fucking asshole he'd been. In the time that they'd been together, Suz had nearly destroyed him, turning him into a kind of whipping boy for her need.

"I thought I'd find you here," Daisy said, taking a seat beside him.

"What's got you looking for me at a damn park

with a bunch of kids?" Crazy glanced over at his friend, seeing the struggle going on inside him. What was wrong with Daisy?

"I'm not in the mood to be around the club whores today."

"Did something happen?" Crazy asked.

"No. Nothing happened, I'm all good. I heard you were with your daughter today, and it has been too damn long since I saw Strawberry."

Crazy laughed. When he was with Suz, he'd stopped Strawberry from visiting the club. He'd not wanted Suz at the club at all. It was bad enough his brothers knew he'd been caught by the evil bitch. "Nah, you can't pull that shit with me. This is you, Daisy. You'd come to my place rather than to the park. What the fuck is going on?"

Silence met his question. Staring at Daisy, he waited, and waited, until finally, Daisy gave in.

"My sister is coming to town to visit."

"So?"

"So, she's bringing her friend, and I've got to put them up."

"Then speak to Duke. He'll make sure they're at the club, and protected."

"That's my fucking problem."

Crazy growled, frustrated with his friend. "What the fuck is your fucking problem?" He had enough problems of his own, and he didn't need to start thinking about Daisy's issues.

"She's bringing her friend, and I want to fuck her. I've known Maria since she was a fucking tomboy kid, but I can tell you, she's not a kid anymore. She's fucking hot, and she hates this life. I can't have her near me."

"Ignore her then."

"I want to fuck her, Crazy. I want to bend her

over in front of the brothers, and fuck her until I brand her with my dick. I don't want any other man to have her. I want to stake my claim, and never let her go. How the fuck am I going to resist that kind of temptation with her close to me?"

Daisy was speaking low enough that only Crazy heard what he was saying. Shit, Daisy didn't just want to get off with Maria. He wanted her as an old lady. That was a big step, a huge one, and it wasn't a decision that was to be taken lightly, or quickly. It had taken Crazy the last couple of months to finally decide to stake a claim on Leanna, the woman who babysat his kid.

He wasn't in the mood right now to think about his woman. Leanna was proving to be … difficult. All of his life he'd snapped his fingers, and bitches had come running to him, and now, he was having to do all the running. The experience wasn't exactly thrilling. He had to do all the hard work. She wouldn't even accept any gifts from him, and refused to go on any dates. How was he supposed to impress a woman when she wouldn't even go on dates?

"Shit, man, I'm sorry. How's it going with Leanna?"

"I'm here alone. How do you think it's going?" Crazy ran a hand down his face. "I'm sorry. It's just hard right now. Strawberry adores her, and she's perfect, and I can't get her to come out with me."

"Have you asked Strawberry to help you?" Daisy asked.

"What do you mean?"

"Get your daughter to invite her out to dinner. Make it an invite from Strawberry rather than an invite from you."

"I'm not going to use my daughter to get the woman I want," Crazy said.

"I wouldn't call it using her. I'd call it 'getting a little help'. Leanna's not going to budge on you."

"She thinks I just want a mom for my kid."

"Don't you?"

Yes, in the beginning what he'd wanted was a mother figure for his little girl. Suz, Strawberry's real mom, had been a piece of shit. She'd used their daughter to keep him in place, turning him into a pussy, and using him for money. Looking back over the last couple of weeks, he realized that he'd been a shadow of his former self. It pissed him off. Suz had turned him into a fucking pussy, and what was worse, he'd let her. No, that shit wasn't happening. He was a fucking man, and he'd put Suz in her place, and she was now gone.

She wasn't dead.

Suz had taken the road of divorce, and getting the fuck out of his life. He was still pissed about that. Crazy had wanted to end her miserable life once and for all. Suz didn't strike him as the settling down kind of woman, or leaving. So far, she'd not come back, and Crazy wasn't going to go looking for trouble.

"We're not talking about me. Let's get back on track here. What's wrong with letting your sister stay, and getting the friend to trust you. It shouldn't be that hard."

Daisy collapsed back against the bench that they were sat at.

"I don't know. Maria is, she's a ball of fire, and if I get too close, I don't know what I'm going to do. No woman should have that kind of power."

Crazy chuckled. "You sound in love."

"I am, Crazy. I'm in love with her, and have been for a long fucking time. The difference is, she's a hell of a lot older now. She could take me on, and fight fire with fire. Beforehand, she was too damn young."

"If you hold out, she may find another man she loves. If that happens, you're never going to reach her. You can force the men to leave her alone, but you can't make her love you. If you want her to love you, then you've got to get past your shit."

Daisy stared out over the park, and Crazy followed his gaze. Strawberry was on a slide, and rushing down it. Her cheeks were bright pink, and the happiness in her face was amazing to witness. Seeing his little girl like this only brought home to him the shit life she'd been in with Suz.

"She's doing good for Suz being gone."

"Yeah, and that's not supposed to be the case." Crazy folded his arms behind his head, and watched his girl. "A girl is supposed to love her mother, not be thinking about other fucking women to take her place. What am I going to do when she's older? It's a woman's place to talk about her cycles, and boys, and sex. Shit, no boy is coming near my little girl. This entire situation is fucked."

"How are things going with Strawberry?" Daisy asked.

"They're going well. I mean, Leanna still takes her when I've got club business to attend to. She's a hoot, she really is." He'd not spent as much time with Strawberry in the last couple of years because the truth was, he couldn't stand to be around Suz. His now ex-wife constantly pissed him off. If only he could get Leanna to start trusting him and not running off every chance she got.

"You know, you should get the club helping your ass," Daisy said.

"Why the fuck would I want the club helping me?"

"Mary, Holly, some of the other old ladies, and

even Zoe, they come across less threatening. They can bring Leanna around, and before you know it, you're fucking her on a daily basis."

"This is going to take more than a couple of women to get what I want."

"Look, I'm helping you out here. No reason to not take the club's help. Sure, the guys won't be that good to you, but the women, they can help. Sheila can help as well. She's been around some time, and knows women."

Crazy ran a hand down his face, pissed off with the fact he may have to get the club women to help him out.

"I wouldn't ask for help off the club whores though. They're more likely to make sure you never get your dick inside that pretty little babysitter."

"The last thing I'm going to do is let Leanna near the women I've put my dick in." They were both speaking quietly so no one heard what they were talking about. Crazy hadn't taken his eyes of his little girl. Vale Valley was a good place, and with the Trojans MC to keep it protected, it rarely had trouble. Crazy wouldn't take any risks with his daughter's life. She was the most precious thing to him, and there were people out there who didn't give a fuck about the threat of being hurt by his club.

Strawberry glanced over at them both at that moment, and squealed. Within seconds she launched herself at Daisy, and Crazy couldn't help but laugh. Due to his daughter's young age, he'd kept her away from the clubhouse. The guys who wanted to could come and visit, but some rarely did. With Holly and Mary recently giving birth, the guys had calmed down their sexual exploits. Not that Crazy could complain. In the last couple of months before he divorced Suz, he'd been using the clubhouse as his own personal sexual drive-thru. He'd take whichever club whore he wanted to have, and fuck her until he was satisfied, then change for another one. Whatever he wanted, he took without care of what others thought. Now, he had his daughter to think about, and a sweet woman who'd go running if she ever caught sight of what went on in the club.

Shit, he had his work cut out for him, but his girl deserved the chance with a woman fit to be called Mom.
****

Leanna walked down the baking aisle in the local supermarket. She had Strawberry that afternoon, and she'd learned the hard way to make sure she always had things to occupy the young girl. Grabbing a box of cake mix from the bottom, she looked at it, turning it over. The mix itself wasn't that great, but if it kept Strawberry happy, then Leanna was happy. When she found one with princesses all over, she picked it up, placing it in the trolley. Then figuring how long she would have the little girl, she placed two more boxes, different kinds, in her trolley.

She was so absorbed in what she was going to do that afternoon that she didn't watch where she was going, and crashed into another cart.

"Crap, I'm so sorry," the woman said.

"No, it's me. I wasn't watching where I was going." Leanna looked up to see Holly, one of the Trojans MC women, holding a baby in her arms.

"I'm Holly by the way."

"I'm Leanna, and I know who you are." Everyone in Vale Valley knew who she was. After all, her old man was now the leader of the Trojans.

"Hols, I got the cake," a young boy said, coming around the corner.

Holly rolled her eyes. "I'm going to make you a

cake, silly. I asked for you to get lots of good quality chocolate, not candy bars."

The boy chuckled. "I was thinking I could eat this on the way home."

"Boys. Sure, put it in. That's Matthew, my lovely, adorable, pain in the ass son."

Seconds later, Matthew was gone. "I'm sorry about that. You're Leanna right? You take care of Strawberry."

Leanna's cheeks heated. She spent a great deal of time trying not to be noticed. Even when she was younger she'd never been the kind of girl who liked crowds, preferring her own company.

"It's nice to meet you."

"You know, you should come to a barbeque one day. We don't bite. I can make sure all the men leave you alone." Holly hiked her son onto her hip.

"It's okay. I'm fine. I'm just getting some things together for Strawberry and me today this afternoon."

The disappointment on Holly's face was clear. The last thing Leanna wanted to do was upset the other woman. She could only imagine Duke coming to her, and yelling at her for hurting Holly, which was the last thing she wanted.

Looking at the little boy on Holly's hip, Leanna smiled. "I want to offer you congratulations on your little boy."

"Thank you. Drake's a few months old now."

"News got around town about his birth. I wanted to say something, or send a gift, but we don't really know each other."

Holly tilted her head to the side. "You do live in Vale Valley, right?"

"All of my life."

"You can come and visit me at the old ranch, or

even at the clubhouse. I don't bite. I can't promise some of the men won't."

Leanna held her hands up. "I'm not very good around people—"

"People or men?" Holly asked, smiling.

Gripping the handle of the trolley, Leanna took a deep breath. "I've never been good at making friends. I'm sorry."

"It's okay. We can take this in little steps. I'm a very nice person, and Matthew will even attest to the fact I'm an excellent stepmom. Also, Drake here is always smiling, and it's not just because he's breaking wind. I come with Mary, and you've got to meet Zoe. She's finishing up college, so she only comes to the clubhouse every once in awhile."

All of the names coming out of Holly's mouth were making Leanna even more nervous. She wasn't good around people or anyone. It was hard having to talk to Crazy, and now that he seemed to always be around with Strawberry, it made her embarrassed. Running fingers through her hair, she glanced over Holly's shoulder. "I appreciate it."

"No, you don't. You want to run far away, and that's okay. Like I said, we can take this in baby steps." Holly tapped her arm. "So, let's go back to the beginning of where we crashed carts, and I will start this."

Leanna frowned as she watched Holly hike her boy up on her hip.

"Hi, I'm so sorry I bumped into you. I wasn't paying attention, and I had Drake here, distracting me. I'm Holly." She held her hand out, and for a second Leanna just looked at it.

This had to be one of the strangest moments of her life. The second strangest moment was when she turned Crazy down. Leanna doubted anyone turned that big scary biker down. Okay, he wasn't all that scary, but she'd seen the way he looked at Suz a couple of times when they'd been together. The guy looked like he wanted to literally strangle his wife. He was sexy, sure, in a very bad boy, "I'm going to kill you" kind of way. No, that wasn't it at all. Crazy was hot. His hair was long, and he hadn't cut it in a couple of months so it rested on his shoulders. Then there were the crazy blue eyes that just captured her attention whenever she was in a room. She loved looking into his eyes. After you got past his eyes, it was his body as well. His arms were covered in tattoos. Some of the ink was just tribal, and dark, others were images of graveyards, and once she witnessed Strawberry's name decorated on his chest. He was a guy who cared deeply for his club, and for his baby.

"Hi, I'm Leanna." She wasn't one of them. Leanna wasn't ever going to be one of those things that he cared about. When he'd started to seduce her, she'd known his intentions. It wasn't like she overheard him or anything. Suz did warn her though after one of her nasty attacks, which Strawberry hadn't witnessed, thank God. Crazy didn't know about the slaps, or hits, and the vile threats that Suz liked to spit at Leanna. She would never allow Suz to hurt Strawberry.

On one of the last visits with Suz, she had been made aware exactly what was going on.

"Crazy's going to try to seduce your fat ass. He doesn't want you. He'll never want you. All he'll ever want is a free babysitter for his little shit of a daughter. Who would want a flubber like you?"

As if on cue, Crazy had been very seductive, talking with her, keeping his focus on her, and she'd seen the reality of her situation. No man was ever going to love her for her. It was always going to be an ulterior motive.

"I've seen you around town, and I know you're Crazy's babysitter. Do you want to get coffee some time?"

"Sure," Leanna said, just wanting to get away. Remembering Suz always did that to her. "I've got to get going."

She looked down into her own trolley to see she still had some stuff to pick up.

"It was nice meeting you."

Without trying to appear rude, she gave the other woman a smile, then made her way up and down the aisles, picking everything she'd need for the coming day. On the way out she saw Holly was being held by none other than Duke. She wondered when he'd come to the grocery store.

Releasing a sigh, she packed her car away, gave Holly a wave, and then drove back home. She parked up in the available parking for her apartment.

Climbing out, she glanced up, and was caught by another couple who were also in some stage of embrace. A jolt of pain pierced her heart at the sight before her. Everyone was in love, and no one was ever going to love her. She'd grown up knowing she wasn't loved, and then married a man who didn't love her, and now, the one man who'd been interested only wanted her for his daughter.

Making her way into her apartment, she started putting away all of her goodies. When it was past one, she heard the knock on her door. Taking a deep breath, she held a box of cake mix, and moved to the door. Plastering on a smile on her face, she opened the door.

"Leanna," Strawberry said, squealing.

The only joy in her life was this little girl, and she held her close.

"How have you been, baby?" She held the little girl tightly to her. Strawberry was so adorable, and Leanna loved her as if she was her own.

"Really good. I saw Daisy at the park."

She chuckled and handed over the cake mix. "We've got a whole afternoon planned."

Another squeal, and Leanna sent her off to wash her hands. Crazy was still inside her apartment. He'd gotten in, and closed the door while she'd been hugging his daughter.

"Hi," she said, folding her arms across her chest.

"Daisy is one of the club brothers."

"Oh, I thought she'd seen an actual daisy at the park."

Crazy laughed. "Nah, he's a brother, but he's got a big ass daisy on his back."

"It's okay. I just won't try to talk to her about flowers." She offered him a smile, and took a step back. It was easier to talk to him if she didn't look at him. Turning her back toward him, she made her way into the kitchen. "Would you like a drink?"

"Yes, I'm not in a rush."

Releasing a sigh, she glanced at the clock, and wished she hadn't extended an invitation toward him.

Chapter Two

Crazy watched the woman he was going to have, to own, as she moved away from him. He'd been at the park with Daisy, talking when he'd gotten the call from Holly to let him know that she'd met Leanna. Holly hadn't been happy with how shy and nervous Leanna had been. What had surprised him was the fact Holly still liked her.

He wasn't fucking happy, and he didn't give a fuck what Holly had to say about her. Crazy was going to do this his way.

"Do you want me to pay for the cake mixes?" he asked, seeing them aligned on her counter.

"No. They didn't cost all that much."

Gritting his teeth, he nodded. She wouldn't let him in, and he was growing tired of fighting her frosty appearance. He'd done a thorough background check on her, and knew she'd been married once.

Taking a seat at the counter, he watched as Strawberry ran into the kitchen. "Can I watch cartoons?"

"We can get started."

"Go and watch cartoons," he said, smiling at his daughter. "I'm just going to have a chat with Leanna."

"Okay, Daddy."

Strawberry left them alone, and he watched Leanna's lips purse. She didn't want to be alone with him. Interesting.

"You've been married before."

She paused and glanced over at him. "You did a check on me?"

Crazy smirked. "You take care of my kid. Of course I did a background check on you." He'd been tiptoeing around her, and he wasn't going to do it anymore. Crazy wasn't known for being meek or a pussy. He was known for loving his pussy, and going after what he wanted. Suz had dampened that part of him, but now he was back, and he was going to take what he wanted, and he wanted Leanna.

"Yes, I was married."

"Where is he?"

"We divorced after a year of marriage."

He knew that as well. What he didn't know was why they'd divorced.

Tilting his head to the side, he watched as she worked in the kitchen, making them both a cup of coffee.

"Do you still need me to take care of Strawberry today?"

"Yes."

"Then why are you still here?"

"You're being very rude."

"I'm not interested in whatever is going on here."

"What is going on?"

"I don't know, Crazy. You tell me." She folded her arms underneath her breasts, staring into his eyes. He couldn't help but look at the rounded sweetness of her tits. They were a fucking dream, and he wanted her naked, underneath him. Her nipples were rock hard, pressing against the front of her shirt. Were her nipples red, brown, pink, large or small? His cock thickened, and he stared down the curve of her body. Leanna was a fucking beautiful woman who hid her curves under clothes that were far too big for her.

"Go out with me."

"No."

He let out a sigh, standing up. Strawberry was watching cartoons, so they would have a little bit of privacy. Rounding the counter, he wasn't surprised when she backed up until she was pressed against the sink.

"You're going to be difficult."

"I'm not going to be a babysitter for you."

Placing his hands on either side of her, he stared into her brown eyes. They were filled with so much pain that at first it took his breath away. Leanna was a mystery, and yet she wasn't. She was a lonely woman that all the men in her life had looked over. Leaning in close, he breathed in the subtle scent of strawberry, and he flicked his tongue against the skin of her neck. She tasted damn good.

"What are you doing?" She went to push him away, but he refused to budge. Being a nice guy wasn't getting him anywhere with Leanna. He was going to have to adapt, and just be the man who always got what he wanted.

"I'm having a little taste of the woman every other guy has overlooked."

"Go away, Crazy. Go and do whatever the hell it is you do, and in a couple of hours, come and pick up your daughter."

"Why did you get a divorce?" he asked, ignoring her instruction.

She was making him harder than any other club whore had ever made him. He'd never sported a dick so hard. Crazy couldn't wait until he got her naked, and he was driving deep into her tight little cunt.

"None of your business."

"You keep no pictures, and you were married before college. Let me guess, the guy used you?"

She took in a startled gasp, and tears filled her eyes. "Leave me alone."

"It's why you're treating me like this. You think I'm only using you as a free babysitter."

"I don't know what you think, but it's lies. Stop trying to analyze me. You're wrong."

He chuckled. "I'm not wrong, and you and I both fucking know it. I'm right, and you're pissed that I am." Placing his hand on her hip, she jumped at the first touch of his body. "You're not a virgin. I bet you had a boring wedding night with that asshole that used you. The doctor, right?"

"Please stop."

"No. I'm not going to stop. I'm starting to believe that everyone in your life has stopped at some point, right? The man you married, the guys you dated, they've all stopped because they had an agenda."

"You have one."

"You're right, I did. I wanted a fucking woman who would spoil my daughter, but what you don't know, Leanna, is I wanted a woman who'd happily suck and ride my dick." When she made to push him away, he caught both of her wrists, and held them against the counter.

"Strawberry will hear you."

"No, she won't. I don't expose my kid to what I want, and I want you, Leanna. I don't just want a babysitter for Strawberry. I want a woman who wants my dick."

"Stop it, and let me go."

"You like what I'm saying to you. I bet you're soaking wet now imagining what it would feel like to have my dick sliding inside you. Are you a virgin?"

"No. I've been married."

"So the bastard used and fucked you. I can end him for you."

She shook her head. He was invading her senses, and with him so close, he saw she was struggling with the closeness. Crazy had found her weakness. She could push him away and ignore him, providing there was space between them. Right now, she couldn't. She was trapped, and that was exactly how he was going to keep her.

"You can't talk like that."

"I am."

"Step back."

"No."

He saw her need to have space. There was no way in hell he was ever going to give her that much space. Crazy had found her weakness, and he was going to use it.

"Has there been any guy who has just wanted you for you?" he asked.

"You don't want me for me. You want me for Strawberry."

Crazy shook his head, and tutted. "I just told you that's not why I want you."

"Then prove it."

Tilting his head to the side, he stared into her defiant eyes. She didn't think he'd be able to prove anything to her. Smiling, Crazy leaned in close so that the hard pressure of his dick was against her stomach.

"I will, but first you've got to make me a promise."

"Back up."

"You've got to promise me that no matter what, you will go out with me. I've got to prove I'm not using you for Strawberry, I will. You've got to make yourself available to me, whenever I want."

"That's crazy."

"It goes with the name, baby. Deal or not."

"No."

"Then how can I meet your challenge?"

She pushed a little harder on his chest trying to get away. He wouldn't budge.

"Fine, I'll meet you any time you want."

"Wherever I want?"

"I'm not a child. If you want to meet somewhere illegal, you can fuck off."

Crazy raised a brow. "It's the first time I heard you curse. You better not be cussing in front of my kid."

"I would nev—"

He silenced her with the press of his lips. "I was teasing, babe."

It was only a mere kiss, a brushing of their lips together, but he wanted more.

"I'll arrange a babysitter tomorrow night. Be free."

He pulled away.

"Wait, you can't."

"I just did."

Crazy gave her a wink before letting himself out of the apartment. He was really looking forward to getting under her skin.

****

Biting her lip, Leanna watched her door open then close, taking the man that had just left her lips tingling along with it.

What was up with Crazy?

She couldn't deal with him being so close, and demanding that she stare at him. Grabbing their cups, she poured the coffee down the sink, and washed away all evidence that she'd even come close to losing it.

He thought she was a virgin?

No, she wasn't a virgin. She gave that up on her wedding night, to the man she really thought she loved, but the truth was, he'd never loved her. No, no one ever loved her. They only wanted her for money.

One of her biggest secrets was the fact she wasn't ever worried about money. She came from a wealthy family, so wealthy she didn't even have to work, but she did, babysitting children in the apartment building. Whenever anyone asked her about her work, she always told them she did her work online. It wasn't that much of a lie. Whenever the family inherited company needed her, she'd deal with it online. There was no need for her input. Her grandfather had made sure that she could be a woman of leisure, without the stress of taking over a company.

Leanna didn't mind. She didn't have it in her to run a company. Running fingers through her hair, she made her way toward the sitting room where Strawberry was. It had been a long running joke in her family that she would have made the perfect wife. Even at a young age nothing gave her more pleasure than being in the kitchen, cooking or baking, and taking care of others. Back then, she'd taken care of her pets. Her grandparents must have seen it, as they made sure she was taken care of.

Her own parents hadn't really wanted much to do with her. They were high flying, living the good life, and with a model as a mother, it hadn't been well known that they had a daughter.

After her parents' deaths in a plane accident while flying toward the Alps for a summer vacation, Leanna had continued to live with her grandparents, as even before their accident, she'd lived with them. She'd been an only child, and her grandparents hadn't liked her parents' celebrity lifestyle, so they had pulled her away from the risk. Through her grandparents, she learned how to respect the money she'd inherit, and to make wise choices. Of course, her first husband had used her as a means to pay for his college education, while she stayed at home. She hadn't known he was using her for money. The knowledge had come to her much later from one of the woman he liked to screw and tell all of his secrets to.

Leanna had never been more embarrassed than when she'd been given proof of his infidelity. They had filmed each other fucking, and Leanna had been forced to watch as he mocked his pathetic fat wife.

Swallowing past the lump in her throat, and the tears that threatened to spill over, she smiled down at Strawberry.

"Are you ready to do those cupcakes now?"

For the rest of the afternoon, her kitchen became a mess with flour, eggs, and mixture decorating all the counters. Strawberry kept on giggling as they finished making the cakes. The mixture wasn't bad, and Leanna had fun. She always had a lot of fun with Crazy's daughter. When the cakes were done and frosted, she let Strawberry eat a cake while she cleaned away all the mess. Humming to herself, she couldn't stop thinking about Crazy, and how he invaded her space.

She'd always been careful and avoided being close to him. The moment he was near, she struggled to think.

What the hell have I done?

There was no way she could go on a date, or even have anything to do with Crazy. The very thought was *crazy*. She needed to put a stop to it before he thought anything could happen between them.

Sitting on the sofa, she watched while Strawberry played with the new coloring book she'd bought for her. She'd always wanted children of her own, a big family, but her wishes had never been granted. After she caught her second boyfriend stealing from her over five years ago, she'd decided against ever having another relationship. She didn't need men to fulfill her life. Moving into this apartment had been a start of a new life for her, one she didn't want to give up. When she'd started babysitting for Strawberry after one of their neighbors told Suz that she did so for free, it had started a need deep inside Leanna.

A need to be the kind of woman that Crazy wanted.

Unknowingly, she'd started to yearn for something she'd not wanted before, a man to want her.

Crazy had awakened the need that she thought had died many years ago.

"Leanna," Strawberry said, crawling up onto the sofa.

"What's the matter, pumpkin?"

"I don't like pumpkins."

"I do. They can be awesome, and I just love pumpkin pie." She pressed a finger to the little girl's nose, smiling. "What did you want to know?"

"Will you be my mommy?"

Her heart broke. There had been no love from Suz for her daughter.

"I can't be your mommy, honey. You've already got a mommy."

"My mommy doesn't like me. She says I was just a thing to get what she wanted."

"I don't know why she wanted you, but your daddy loves you."

Strawberry's smile widened. "I love my dad."

"Good."

"Do you love my dad?"

"I don't know your dad well enough, honey. Come on, it's time for some food."

She took her hand, and made her way back into the kitchen. Soon Strawberry was talking about the latest movie she wanted to see, and about Daisy playing in the park. Leanna was thankful for the distraction.

There was no way she had any feelings for Crazy. In fact, the moment he came to pick her up tonight, she was going to tell him not to bother. Any guy like Crazy wouldn't be worth the risk to her heart. She'd had her heart broken several times, but Crazy had the power to smash it to smithereens. Leanna didn't want to be at the mercy of the sexy, dangerous biker.

She'd avoided anything to do with the Trojans MC. They had a reputation in town for being wild, and she'd heard several of the women bragging about their ability to fuck. Just the thought of Crazy naked, wanting to be inside her, had heat sweeping her pussy. She got wet instantly thinking about him, and what he was capable of.

Later that night, Strawberry fell asleep on her bed, and she closed the door so nothing would wake her.

By the time Crazy knocked on her door, she had already practiced what she was going to say to him. She would make it clear to him in no uncertain terms that there was no chance of anything happening between them.

Rubbing her sweaty palms across her thighs, she opened the door, and gasped. He was wearing his leather jacket, his hair swept back off his face, and looking too hot for his own good. All of her excuses filled her throat causing an imaginary lump to form in her throat.

"We can't—"

She didn't get to say anything else as he pushed into her apartment. He closed the door, pressing her up against him. There was not one part of her that wasn't touching him, and she couldn't find the strength to push him away. She didn't want to.

"I knew you'd find a reason not to come out with me."

"It's for the best."

Crazy shook his head. "It's not for the best. You set a challenge, and I'm going to prove it to you. Holly and Mary are taking care of Strawberry tomorrow night. I'm dropping her off at the ranch, and you're coming on a date with me."

"No."

"Yes. Be ready at seven or I take what I want here."

"You can't do this. You can't force me to go on a date with you." She finally found the strength to push him away.

It didn't work.

Crazy refused to budge, and it annoyed the hell out of her. She couldn't think if he was this close, and it was frustrating her.

"Go out with me, or tomorrow night I will come here, and I will fuck you to make you forget about all the men who've used you. I swear to you, baby, you're going to go on a date with me, one way or the other. I'm done with you hiding."

Chapter Three

"Are you sure you're okay with this?" Crazy asked, making his way toward the door.

"Mary and I can handle your daughter. We've got kids of our own," Holly said. "Go and have fun on your date."

He wasn't nervous about his date, but he was about leaving Holly and Mary alone with his kid. Sure, the two women were the best of friends, but they were both little hell-fires when they got started. He didn't want his little girl to start fighting with him because he was not an empowered woman or some shit.

"Don't corrupt my girl."

Mary laughed, walking around the corner, holding her own daughter. She had given birth two months ago to a squealing baby girl. Pike was completely in love with his woman, and daughter, and they made for a very happy family. "Strawberry was corrupted the moment you brought her through that door. We're going to tell her who really is boss. Girls do everything better."

Rolling his eyes, he let himself out the door.

"You can count on us, Crazy. We'll have her hunting, making explosives, and doing my famous kick to the balls move," Holly said.

"God help me," he said, the moment the door closed.

Holly and Mary were both amazing, fun women to be around. Duke and Pike were lucky men, but then so was Raoul, who'd recently married Zoe, the young woman he'd saved from being gang raped.

It amazed Crazy at times how much shit could happen in so little time. It had been over a year since Holly and Duke had married, yet it had felt like years with how natural they all were.

Climbing into Duke's car, which he borrowed for his date, he drove toward the apartment blocks where he and Leanna lived.

She was going to find some excuse to avoid him and their date. He was thankful he now knew her weakness. All he had to do was invade her space, crowd her with his presence, and she became putty in his hands. He would be lying if he was to say that he didn't like it. He did. Crazy fucking loved her response to him.

Someone who couldn't think around him wouldn't be able to turn away, or turn him down. He intended to use it all to his advantage. Climbing out of the car, he was swinging the keys between his fingers, and whistled as he made his way up toward her room.

Knocking on the door, he waited.

Leanna opened, and his cock went into overdrive. He'd rarely seen her in clothes that actually fit to her body. She wore a pair of jeans that melded to her thick hips and thighs, and a shirt that gathered in at her waist, but highlighted her generous tits.

Out of all of the women, club whores and old ladies, Leanna's tits were the best, and biggest. His mouth watered at just the thought of a taste. He wanted her naked, under him, and riding him. Fuck, he just wanted her, and he didn't give a fuck what it was going to take to get her.

His cock was throbbing with need, and he no longer wanted to go out on a date.

"You're not going to fight me?" he asked, disappointed. He wanted any excuse to have her hands all over him.

"I don't want to stay here."

She grabbed her purse, and before he knew what was happening, they were outside of her apartment.

Okay, she may have figured out her one weakness without him. It was now up to him to take the next step.

"Come on, beautiful." He took her hand, leading her down to the car.

"I didn't know you had a car."

He waited for her to climb into the car, and with other women, he'd have left them to place the seatbelt across themselves, but with Leanna, he did it. Brushing the back of his fingers across her breasts, he had to stifle a moan at the softness of them. She really was a beautiful, soft woman.

Closing the door, he took a breath, and tried to think of anything that would lessen the stiffness in his cock. Nothing was helping. If anything, he was only getting harder. He needed to think, not have all thought go to his dick.

"Where are we going?" she asked, running her hands down her thighs.

"We're going to have some dinner, and some dancing."

"I can cook for us, or you can go for take out."

"You're trying to separate us?" He turned toward her, giving her his full attention.

"What? No, not at all."

"We're going to dance, and eat."

Turning the ignition over, he started out of the parking lot, heading away from Vale Valley. The bar he knew was just on the outskirts of the city.

"Should we be going to a bar with you driving?"

"I'm not going to be drinking. I'm responsible, Leanna."

She was silent for several seconds, and he chanced a glance over at her to find that she was biting her lip.

"What are you thinking about?" he asked.

"I'm just curious about what happened to Suz. Strawberry said she'd not seen her for some time."

Tightening his hands around his steering wheel, Crazy tried to control his temper. "Are you trying to put distance between us by bringing up my ex-wife?"

"No, you're divorced?"

"Yes, I'm divorced. I never loved Suz. I fucking hated the bitch. She was a club whore, and had more dick than any other fucking woman. The only reason I married her was because of Strawberry."

"You don't have to marry in this day and age," Leanna said. Her voice was small.

"I wasn't going to give Suz the chance of taking my kid from me. She'd do it as well. Suz only cared about herself, and if it hurt me, then she'd have put Strawberry up for adoption, or even killed her." Crazy didn't want to be thinking about his ex. He had a tendency to want to murder the slut.

"I'm sorry. I didn't mean to pry." Leanna sat back in her seat.

Crazy cursed inwardly, and released the steering wheel. He kept hold of the wheel, but he no longer had it in a death grip.

"It's okay. I didn't expect the topic to be all that fun."

"I'm not very good around people, or anyone. It's not your fault that you picked a dud."

"Don't fucking do that," he said, cursing. "Don't put yourself down. Damn, those bastards really did a number on you."

Again, silence filled the car.

"It was my own fault," she said, after a couple of seconds had passed. "I didn't stand up, and make it stop. I let it all happen."

"We're not always responsible for what happens

to us."

"I know that, but it's up to ourselves on how we react to what actually happened. I didn't handle it well."

Releasing a sigh, Crazy glanced over at her. "I don't want to ruin this date."

"This is a date?"

"Yes, it's a date, and it's not because of a challenge either."

"You do realize dating each other doesn't change what you want from me."

Crazy didn't talk as he saw the parking lot to the bar up ahead. Pulling into the back of the lot, he parked the car. He preferred being at the back of the lot as it was so much easier to get out at the end of the night.

"How does it not change anything?"

"You still want me to take care of Strawberry."

"I can stop you caring for my kid in a heartbeat. The club is full of old ladies who'll do whatever I want, including help take care of Strawberry."

She bit her lip.

"Do you want that?" he asked.

She shook her head. "I like her."

"I'm going to take you out on dates, and we're going to spend time with Strawberry together, but I'm not going to dump my kid on you, and go fucking everything else. I'm going to prove to you, I want you for a hell of a lot more than just the mother for my kid."

"What does Suz think about that?"

"She's been gone nearly six months, and not once gotten in touch. What do you think? I couldn't even get her to love Strawberry when she was in my life." Climbing out of the car, he rounded to her side, and opened the door. Taking her hand, he pulled her up close, slamming the door closed. Pressing her against the body of the car, he cupped her hip, showing her how hard he was as his cock pushed against her stomach. "That's how much I want you, and believe me, I'm not thinking about my kid with this."

No, he was thinking about getting Leanna naked underneath him, and finding out how soft her curves were.

Dropping a kiss to her lips, he smiled as she went in for a deeper kiss but he pulled back. Getting Leanna was going to take some time.

Making their way into the bar, he didn't give her a chance to pull away from him, taking her straight to the bar. He ordered himself a soda, and Leanna a wine. She needed to loosen up a little.

"I don't drink. Can I have an orange soda?" she asked.

"Bring it to our table, Dan." He led her toward the back of the booth away from everyone.

"Why are we in this bar?" she asked.

"This is a damn good place. There's no drugs, and there's no shit. It's adults only, but it's a place to eat good food and dance." He pointed toward the dance-floor close to their table. Dan, the owner, had made sure to keep enough space between the booths, and the dance floor. "So why don't you drink?"

****

This date was not going how Leanna had hoped. She'd intended to put Crazy off, and that meant talking about Suz, and everything that would make for a bad experience.

Biting her lip, she stared down at her hands that were locked together at the table.

"So, why don't you drink?"

Hating his question, she knew there was no point in keeping that crap to herself. "I was drunk when I accepted the proposal from my first husband."

"And?"

"And if I wasn't drunk, I may have seen through his proposal."

Crazy's brow was raised. "Are you telling me that you spent most of your marriage drunk?"

"No."

"Then drink wasn't the reason you were blind to him."

"I don't want to talk about this." She tucked her hands back into her lap.

"They always take a little bit from us, don't they?" he asked.

She waited for their drinks to be placed in front of them along with the menus. Crazy thanked Dan, and they were alone. "Who take what from us?"

"Ex-partners, lovers, they come and take a little of us in whatever form they can."

Taking a sip of the cool soda, she returned her gaze back to him. "What did Suz take from you?"

"My spunk."

She choked on her drink, and stared at him wide eyed. "Wow, you don't even sugarcoat it, do you?"

"You're determined to make this a bad date. I'm not going to pretend I haven't fucked my fair share of women. I've fucked a lot of women, a lot of pussy. Suz was a mistake. I couldn't stand her. She broke the condom on purpose, and yes, she took my spunk that wasn't freely given. What about you? What did those bastards do to you?"

"This isn't a date—"

"You wanted this for your line of questioning." He leaned forward taking hold of hand. "We'll get all of our shit on the table now, and later on, we'll not have anything to hide."

Leanna felt guilty. "I wanted this to go awfully."

"I've fucked a lot of women, Leanna. Suz got herself knocked up because she tampered with the condom."

"Were you faithful to her?"

"In the beginning I was. The last couple of months, I didn't give a shit. I fucked some of the women at the club, who open their legs for all of the brothers."

Taking a sip of her drink, Leanna stared into his eyes. He was telling the truth.

"I'm not going to cheat on you. We're dating, and I'm going to prove to you that I can be the man for you."

She believed him. Crazy wasn't known for being a liar.

"I've not been with anyone in three years. I decided I wasn't going to allow myself to trust anyone," she said.

"You can trust me. I'm going to prove it to you. The club is free sexually. We fuck who we want, when we want, and we don't always do it behind closed doors."

"What about Duke and Pike?"

"They are monogamous to their women. I've never seen either of them with anyone else since claiming Mary and Holly."

She smiled. "I noticed you said since they've been with Mary and Holly."

"We're men who don't hide our need. We love to fuck."

"You're blunt. I think you're the bluntest man I've known."

"I don't believe in pussy footing around." He reached over, taking her hand once again, and turning it over, running his fingers over her pulse. "Like now, I'm curious about the color of your nipples. Are they red, brown, pink?"

Heat filled her cheeks, and she fought the urge to pull away. All of the men she'd been with before Crazy looked weak compared to him.

Fight fire with fire.

You want him.

Have him, and leave your heart out of it.

Leanna had never been the kind of woman who had a man chasing after her. The kind of men she'd been with were the ones who liked to keep the light off when they had sex, and it was always the missionary style. It had taken her stumbling on a porn site to find there was more than one way to have sex.

She'd wanted to have dirty, sweaty, hot sex, at least once.

Was Crazy the best man to discover it with?

Yes.

Leaning forward, she didn't pull her hand away, she stared into his eyes. "I have red nipples, and they're large, not small."

You can do this.

Crazy's eyes grew wide, and she was happy to have finally caught him unaware.

"You see, now I just want to see them."

Licking her dry lips, she turned his arm over, and traced inside his wrist. The word "Freedom" was inked on the inside.

"You been in prison?"

"I did a stint about fifteen years ago when I was twenty. I got caught on a weapons' charge. I did my time, and that was it. I promised myself I wouldn't go back inside."

Tracing the word with the tip of her finger, she wondered what kind of man he would have been before he went inside.

"I couldn't handle prison."

"No, you couldn't."

He didn't pull away from her, but she knew that was it.

Crazy wasn't going to tell her anything more about his life on the inside.

"You're curious." He traced a line up the inside of her arm.

"Yes." She was in no doubt as to what he was asking. Leanna was curious about him, and what he could give her. There was no way she needed to have a relationship with him for what she wanted. She could take care of Strawberry, find out what all the fuss was about in the bedroom, and keep her heart intact.

"I know what you're trying to do," he said, sitting back.

"I'm not trying to do anything."

"If you're curious about having sex, I can help you with that. If you think for a second you're going to use me, you're wrong."

"You were going to use me."

"Past tense. I can fuck you until the next millennium, and have you spending days wondering how many orgasms you actually had, but don't for a second think you can use me. I'm not the kind of man to be used."

Shoulders slumping, she jolted as he climbed out of the booth. He didn't move away, and urged her up so that he was sitting beside her. The wall stopped her from going anywhere else.

He placed his arm across her shoulders, and with the other, he cupped her cheek.

"No one can see."

"How did you know what I was thinking?"

"I've seen your mind working, and it's not hard to guess." He traced his thumb across her lips, and slipped it down her neck. She expected him to stop, but he didn't. Moving down to her shirt, he tugged it down.

"What are you doing?"

"No one will see. I'm here, and you're covered. Anyone else will think we're having a private conversation."

She kept her hand over his, and stared into his eyes.

"Try to look over my shoulder."

Leanna tried to look but couldn't see anyone. Crazy had her covered.

Slowly, she released his hand. He tugged the neckline of her shirt down until her bra covered breast was exposed. Crazy removed the bra, and finally he broke eye contact with her. His gaze moved to her nipple.

Heat filled her pussy, making her grow slick with arousal.

"Are you wet?"

"Yes."

"I know you are, baby. Your nipple is hard, showing me that you want my dick. Your body is more honest than those lips of yours. Don't worry, I'll have them wrapped around my dick soon enough."

She bit her lip to stop herself from snapping at him. He flicked his finger over her exposed nipple, and she couldn't believe she was allowing this to happen. His touch was lighting a fire deep inside her, and she was scared that there was not going to be anything but him that could put it out. This was why she'd tried to keep him at arm's length. Crazy had the power to make her lose control, and only focus on the need.

"When we're alone, I'm going to suck these tits until you're almost coming. We're going to have a lot of fun together."

He tucked her breast back inside, and leaned down to brush her lips with a kiss. She didn't fight him. There was no point in fighting him. Everything he was doing to her, she wanted. Leanna had simply been denying herself whereas others didn't.

Chapter Four

Their meal went a lot better after he invaded her space, touching her body every chance he got. There was a side to Leanna that she'd kept well guarded from him, and he imagined from the outside world.

Crazy couldn't believe he'd not seen it before now.

There was a wildness inside her, and he was going to draw her out.

"Let's dance."

They had shared a platter of wings and hot sauce. He wasn't near full, but he wanted to give Leanna all the experience she wanted.

Taking her hand, he moved toward the dance-floor. The heavy beat had him holding her hands and swaying to the music.

"I don't dance," she said.

Tugging her in close, he slid a thigh between her legs and took her hips in his hands. "It's not about listening to the music, but your body."

Her hands wrapped around his neck, and he held her close while taking her on a dance. She was such a sensual, sexy woman. Rocking her hips from side to side, he stared into her eyes.

His cock thickened as her soft body pressed against his own. Her tits were beautiful, and he couldn't wait to get his mouth on them, or even have them pressed around his dick.

"Are you having fun?"

She started to relax, and follow his lead with the music.

"Yes. This has been a lot of fun."

"Don't sound so surprised."

She laughed. "This has to be the first date I've actually ever had fun, and we've gotten all of our crap out on the table."

"I'm not going to hide from you, or the club."

"You make it sound like one big orgy."

"Some nights, it is, and yes, I've participated."

She started to play with the hairs at the back of his neck. "You need to get a haircut."

Crazy gripped her ass tightly, sliding his hand down the crease closing in on her pussy.

"Crazy?"

"Follow me."

He took her hand, and led her down a long corridor. Crazy couldn't last another second. Pressing her against the wall, he slammed her wrists above her head, and took possession of her mouth.

She tasted of spice and the orange soda she'd been drinking. It was a heady combination, and one he wanted more of. Leanna gasped, and he slid his tongue in, locking her hands above her head, as he used his other to slide down her body.

"Do you want to play with me, Leanna?"

"Yes."

"Then I think it's safe to have some ground rules."

"More rules?"

"You're the one who wanted me to prove that I wanted to date you for you. I'm doing that." He glided his hand down until he cupped her pussy through her jeans. "You don't hide from me. Strawberry doesn't need to know that we're dating, and fucking."

"I've not said I'm fucking you."

He groaned. "Damn, you're going to do a lot of talking when my dick is inside you, sliding in your tight cunt."

She gasped but didn't push him away. There was a fire inside Leanna, and he was going to unleash it.

"We're going to fuck, and you're going to love every second of it. I'll give you everything you want, and I'll take it."

He nibbled down to her neck, sucking on her flesh. "Deal?"

"You touch another woman, it's off."

"Deal."

Slamming his lips back on hers, Crazy sealed the deal. Once he finished kissing her, he didn't give her a chance to catch her breath. He moved toward the bar, paid their bill, and had her back in his car, strapped in, and was heading back to their apartment before she could utter a word of protest.

"You're acting crazy."

"I want what I want." He took her hand, locking their fingers together. Crazy didn't let her go until he parked the car in their parking lot. Leanna climbed out of the car before he got the chance to go 'round to her side. He wrapped his arms around her waist, and followed behind her.

Leanna's hands were shaking as she tried to find the key. He wondered how many men had led her back to her apartment, intent on fucking their brains out.

The evening hadn't started out with him wanting to fuck her, but it was going to end with his dick deep in her pussy.

Opening the door, he pushed her inside, and slammed the door closed. Grabbing her arm, he shoved her up the wall. His actions created noise, but he wasn't hurting her.

Without waiting for her permission, he shoved her shirt up, over her head.

"You were enticing me tonight."

"You asked."

"Now I'm going to taste." He snapped the catch of her bra, and her large tits sprang free. Cupping her tits in his hands, he ran his thumb across each hardened nipple. She gasped, thrusting her chest out to him. "That's right, push them up to me. I'm going to spend a great deal of time with these beauties."

Leaning forward, he flicked his tongue over one extended nipple, and sucked it deep into his mouth.

She cried out at the same time as he moaned.

Leanna tasted a lot better than he ever imagined. Sliding his tongue across her chest, he lavished attention to her other nipple. With his mouth at work, he flicked the catch on her jeans, and began pushing them down her hips.

"We should talk about this."

"I'm done talking." Slipping his hand inside her panties, he started to finger her slick cunt. "You're wet for me, baby. You've been holding out on me, and I'm not going to let you do that anymore." Biting her nipple, he watched the rapture cross her face, and knew there was a little slut inside Leanna. All he needed to do was push the right buttons, and she'd belong to him.

Suz had been a slut to the core, fucking every single man around. Leanna was different. She would be his little slut, and no one else would ever know what she was like.

Sliding two fingers inside her, he groaned as her pussy clenched around his fingers, and he added a third finger. He wanted his dick inside her, and the worse for him, he didn't want to wear a condom. Crazy was clean, and he just knew that Leanna would be.

"I want to fuck you."

Sucking her nipple into his mouth, he released it with a plop, and stepped back. He didn't give her enough space, and removed his clothes so that he was standing before her, naked. It didn't take him long. He needed to relieve the pressure from around his dick.

Wrapping his fingers around his cock, he stared into her eyes. "You see this?"

She nodded.

"This is what you do to me. This has nothing to do with my kid. This is all you, Leanna. Every time I'm close to you, I want to fuck you." Taking hold of her hand, he wrapped her fingers around his length.

He ran his thumb across the tip that was leaking pre-cum, and placed it on her lips. "Taste me."

She flicked her tongue out, and he almost came there and then. It was the most erotic sight he'd ever seen, and in all of his years of fucking, it was saying something.

"You're going to have me begging aren't you?"

"I'm not very experienced." She squeezed his dick a little tighter.

"Don't worry. We'll teach each other." Sinking his fingers into her hair, he led her toward the couch. There was no time to go anywhere else. They'd make it to a bed at some point, just not now.

He dropped her to the couch, following down with her.

Leanna's body was a fucking dream, soft in all the right places. She filled his hands to perfection, and he couldn't imagine having another woman beneath him. Her tits bounced and shook with each of her indrawn breaths. He'd hated Suz with her slender, skeleton body. Crazy understood what Duke, Pike, and Raoul saw in their women. They were all larger women, and they made a man want to come home at night.

Plunging his tongue into her mouth, he claimed the kiss he'd been wanting since he'd come to collect her. He wasn't going to hold back anymore with Leanna. Crazy wouldn't go against her rules in front of Strawberry, but the moment his kid was not around, Leanna belonged to him.

Breaking from the kiss, he trailed his lips down her neck, to her breasts. Sucking each nipple back into his mouth, Crazy cupped them together, slipping his tongue between the globes. "I'm going to fuck you here, and you're going to love it."

"Please."

"Sh." He didn't linger on her tits even though he wanted to. They were so amazing. He was going to spend many hours fucking them. Kissing down her stomach, he dipped his finger into her belly button, before moving down. Opening her thighs, he stared at her creamy cunt, and his mouth watered. He would never grow bored of licking this woman out.

****

Crazy was surrounding every part of her. Any sense that Leanna had once had, disappeared the moment he started touching her. This was why she tried to keep him at arm's length. He wasn't like any of the other men she'd been with. He was just … male. Not one part of him was weak. Crazy wasn't afraid or ashamed of who he was, and what he liked, taking and giving with equal measure.

Glancing down at where he was looking, Leanna bit her lip. He was staring at her pussy.

He moved down, sliding the lips of her sex open, and Leanna gasped as he quickly licked from her entrance to her clit. Crying out, she fell to the couch only to rise up as he plundered her pussy with his tongue. There was no way a man was supposed to know how to make a woman beg. It wasn't fair. Gripping the edge of her couch, she groaned.

She'd have to wash the fabric. Her cream leaked out of her pussy, dripping down the crack of her ass, and she guessed onto the couch.

"You taste fucking perfect."

Groaning, she started to thrust up to meet his tongue. His fingers went from teasing her clit, to slamming inside her, switching with his tongue.

Her orgasm grew and grew, startling her with how quickly she went to the edge.

"That's it, give it to me."

He bit on her clit. Pain exploded at the same time as pleasure with his fingers stroking over her G-spot, at just the right angle.

Screaming out, Leanna crashed into her orgasm, taken completely off guard by the intense pleasure. Crazy didn't stop there. He prolonged her orgasm until she couldn't take it anymore.

Crazy moved up, and over her body.

Placing her hands on his chest, she paused.

"I'm not leaving with blue balls."

"You need to get a condom. I'm not protected. I could get pregnant."

He jumped over the couch, and within a second, he was rolling a condom on with such efficiency that she didn't want to think about it. Crazy moved between her thighs, aligned the tip of his cock to her core, and was about to slam home when his cell phone rang.

Leanna groaned. "Forget about it," she said.

"I can't."

There was Strawberry to think about, and for a split second, she had forgotten. Crazy cursed, and pulled away. His cock was still rock hard, and Leanna sat up. With each step he took, her mind grew clearer. Most times, she saw the danger she was in, giving herself to Crazy. He had a lot of power, the power to break her heart, and crush her in ways no man had. Only this time, she didn't see the danger as she looked at him. She saw the pleasure to be had, the fun. All of the kinds of fun she'd wanted from her husband, and the boyfriends she'd had.

"Hello. Shit. She okay? No, I'll come and get her." Crazy disconnected the call.

Grabbing a pillow, Leanna placed it in front of her. "What's the matter?"

"Strawberry's sick. She's thrown up her dinner, and I need to go pick her up. Holly was more than happy to keep her, but she was calling for me."

"Duty calls."

Crazy placed his phone on the coffee table, and sat beside her. She moaned as he sank his fingers into her hair, and pressed his lips to hers. "Crazy?"

"I've got to go, baby. I promise you I'll be back."

"I was the one that got off."

"And you're going to be the one making sure I get off when the time is right." He pressed another kiss to her lips, and groaned. "If I didn't have to go I'd be deep within your pussy right now."

This was her time to groan. "Don't say things like that."

"It makes you wet. You love it."

She touched his cheek, and pressed her face to his. "Stop."

"You're right. I've got to go."

He stood up, moving around the back of the couch toward the pile of clothes. Unable to just sit there, Leanna followed him, tugging on her underwear, and clothes.

I don't want him to go.

Gripping her shirt, she stared at him, biting her lip. "Would you like me to come with you?"

"Nah, I wouldn't expect that from a date. Strawberry is sick, so it's going to be a bad sight."

"I'm not asking as your date." I'm asking as your woman. See, this is what you get when you try to be a smart ass. "I'm asking as your friend."

"You don't have to come."

"I know, and that's one of the reasons why I do want to come."

He released a sigh, and nodded. "Only if you want to come. I'm not going to force you."

"I'm coming. I don't like the thought of Strawberry being ill."

They finished getting dressed. Leanna followed him down to the car, and it wasn't long before they were in front of Holly's house. She saw the concern he had for his daughter, and it made her care about him just a little bit more.

She'd never been to the ranch before. The moment she saw it, Leanna fell in love with it. It was a large house, beautiful, and the views were beyond compare as it overlooked the many landscapes outside of Vale Valley.

"She's on the couch," Holly said, opening the door.

Following behind Crazy, she bit her lip as Holly gave her a smile on the way out of the door.

"I hope I didn't interrupt your date."

"It's fine." Her cheeks heated, and Leanna saw the gleam in the other woman's eyes. Crap, just once she'd love for her body not to respond to a knowing look.

"Strawberry's been asking for you and her dad."

Moving into the sitting room, Leanna saw Mary sat across from the little girl looking worried.

"Duke took Michael on a camping trip, and Pike had to run an errand for the club," Holly said. "I didn't know what else to do, and she was wanting you both."

"Both?" Leanna said.

The moment the little girl saw her, her eyes lit up. Strawberry rushed off the couch, throwing herself at her. Picking her up, Leanna held her close, feeling her temperature.

"We better get you home. She probably picked something up at the park." They grabbed her stuff, said goodbye to the women, and made their way back to the car. She sat in the back, holding Strawberry close while Crazy drove. It was a little after ten by the time they made it to Crazy's apartment. She carried Strawberry to her room, sitting down with her, and rubbing her back.

She loved how natural it was for her and Crazy to take care of Strawberry. Another hour had passed by the time Strawberry fell asleep. Crawling out from beneath her arms, she walked behind Crazy as they made it to the sitting room.

In the months that Suz had been gone, the apartment had transformed. She'd always been shocked at the bland, almost dank look of the place. Crazy had changed the furniture, giving it a more modern look. The walls were decorated cream, and the ceilings white.

"You think she caught something at the park?"

"Other kids are there, and if they're poorly, it doesn't take long to spread." She shrugged, pressing the back of her hand to her mouth.

"Shit, you're tired."

"I'm going to head home. I really enjoyed tonight."

She was passing him, and he caught her arm. "Don't leave."

"Crazy?"

"I've got a bed. We don't have to fuck, and this isn't about Strawberry. I'll make sure I get up for her. I just, I don't want this night to end, and I want to be with you."

Unable to deny him, she nodded, and followed him toward the bedroom.

"I changed the bed, and the mattress. I didn't want to be on anything that Suz had touched."

"You wiped all trace of her out of the apartment."

"I'm looking for a house, but I've yet to find anything suitable. I want to give Strawberry a place that she loves."

He moved to some drawers at the end of the room.

Crazy turned around holding up a shirt. "You can wear this. The bathroom is across the hall."

She took the shirt from him. "I'm just going to wash up."

Standing in Crazy's shower, Leanna closed up at the spray of water, and moaned as the heat ran down her body. They lived in a decent apartment building, so they rarely ever had to worry about no water.

The night's events ran through her mind, and she pressed a hand between her thighs, touching her pussy. She wanted Crazy inside her.

Stop, Leanna.

Removing her hand, she finished getting washed, and found the nearest towel, wiping the water from her eyes. Crazy was sitting at the end of the bed when she returned wearing his shirt.

"How do I look?"

"You look fucking hot."

She gave a smile, and suddenly needed to yawn.

"Time for bed."

He pulled the blanket back. "I'll be back in a moment."

Climbing into bed, she ran her hands over the

bed. Looking at his pillow, she grabbed it, and inhaled his masculine scent. It smelled like him, and the scent calmed her.

I'm lying in Crazy's bed, sniffing his pillow like a damn dog.

If Suz saw her now, the other woman would laugh at her.

Lying down on the bed, she didn't have to wait long for Crazy to join her. His hair was wet as he lay down, and for several seconds they looked at each other.

He touched her cheek, stroking a finger over her lips.

Words were not needed, and Leanna closed her eyes, finding sleep.

Chapter Five

Daisy stared at his phone as he sat at the bar. The Friday night fuck-fest had already moved on upstairs, and the only pussy waiting around the bar was tired, used up pussy. Flicking open his phone, he stared down at the picture of his sister, Beth, and her best friend Maria.

His sister was a beauty. Blonde hair, blue eyes, and she had the girl–next-door look. She was sweet, charming, and he knew guys would want to fuck her. Daisy wasn't an asshole. He didn't like the thought of any bastard being near his sister, but he wasn't a hypocrite. Maria, however, was the woman who held his attention. She had long, raven hair, and in this photograph she'd just turned nineteen. His sister had taken it and sent it to him.

He had a good friendship with his sister, and he adored her.

"What's got you looking like a bitch has refused to suck your dick?" Knuckles asked, taking a seat beside him.

"My sister, Beth. She's supposed to be stopping by for the summer."

Knuckles whistled. "Sweet."

"Don't."

"I take it your sister isn't the reason you're looking all troubled."

Gritting his teeth, Daisy took a sip of his drink.

"No, she's not."

Knuckles knocked on the counter, and clicked his tongue. "Okay, I'm guessing that sweet piece of ass is the reason you've been miserable, and acting like a pussy."

"I've not been acting like a pussy."

"Dude, you've been acting like a pussy, and everyone knows it."

Slamming his hand down on the counter, Daisy was about to leave, but Knuckles pushed him back down. "Sit the fuck down."

"I don't have to take fucking orders from you."

"I'm not here to give you orders. I'm here to offer a piece of advice, or at the least, the option of talking to you."

"You've got nothing to say to me that will make me feel better."

"I'm not here to make you feel better. I'm here to put some reality to your trouble." Knuckles grabbed the whiskey bottle from behind the counter.

"There is no reality."

"Yeah, there is. You've got yourself all worked up on a woman who might not even like you."

"Maria doesn't like me."

"Are you going to force yourself on a woman?"

"No. I'd never do that." Daisy was repulsed at the thought of forcing himself on a woman. He didn't believe in rape to take what he wanted. There was more than enough willing pussy to take in the club.

"Then you could be worried about Maria, and she might have a boyfriend of her own, or not even have a crush on you, or anything. Get your head out of your ass, be a big brother, and for fuck's sake, stop moping. You're giving our club a bad name."

Rolling his eyes, Daisy snatched the bottle out of his hand. Knuckles had put a little perspective on his problem. He was supposed to take care of Maria and Beth. There was no need to start worrying about what was expected of him.

He liked variety in his pussy.

"I have to say, Beth sure is a sweet pussy. She

53

seeing anyone?"

"You're not getting anywhere near my sister, asshole."

He'd fucked many women with Knuckles. The very thought of his sweet sister with a man like Knuckles made him shudder.

Heading upstairs to his room, he saw Bee coming out of Pie's room. Wrapping his arms around her waist, he picked her up over his shoulder, and carried her toward his room. Bee released a squeal, and he slapped her ass.

"You coming, Knuckles? I found a cunt that is in need of a couple of dicks." Bee groaned, and the scent of her pussy was easy to detect.

He loved sweet-butts. They were just so fucking easy, and they didn't require any work. All of the sluts hanging around the club didn't make any of the brothers work for it, and he loved them all for that. It made it so easy to share them, and move on. Bee had already taken her share of club dick.

Maria.

Daisy knew she'd be a virgin.

He didn't have time to train a virgin.

Dropping Bee to the bed, he slid his fingers into her cunt. She was loose as fuck, but his dick was big enough to fill her pussy. Her ass hadn't been used all that much. He'd take that, and it would tighten her cunt enough for Knuckles.

****

Crazy opened his eyes and stared at Leanna's sleeping face. She looked so peaceful, and he'd promised her he wouldn't wake her up. Strawberry had woken up three times through the night, vomiting.

She wanted Leanna, but he'd made her promise not to wake her up.

Last night had been the best, and worst, of his life. He lifted some hair off her face, and watched as she snuggled a little closer to him.

"What am I going to do about you?"

What had started out as a way of finding a babysitter for his kid, had turned into something else.

Leanna had the power to get under his skin and into his heart. He didn't like it, and didn't even want to think about it.

Sliding out of the bed, he made his way to the bathroom. After taking a piss and washing his hands, he splashed some water over his face. Staring at his reflection, Crazy saw a man he'd not seen for a long time. He looked somewhat sane. Running a hand down his face, he cleared the remaining sleep.

"Do you like her? Do you love her?"

He liked Leanna. Did he love her? Crazy enjoyed being around her, but last night had shown him that he didn't really know anything about her.

Leaving the bathroom, he made his way toward Strawberry's room.

His little girl was sitting on the floor, playing with her dolls.

"How are you feeling?"

"Better."

Sitting down on the floor, he picked up a doll, and started talking in a girly voice. Strawberry laughed, moving to sit on his lap.

"Daddy, do you love Leanna?"

"Yes."

"Will you get married, and turn her into a princess?"

Crazy smiled. "You think I've got the power to turn her into a princess?"

"Yes. When you marry a girl, she's a princess."

Kissing her head, he watched her playing for several seconds.

"I like Leanna. I really like her. Will you be a good girl, and invite her out to dinner with us today?"

"Do I get ice cream?"

"Are you bargaining with me?"

"I've got school. I need to learn."

"Half a night with Holly and Mary, and you're bartering with me. Yes, you will get ice cream."

"A toy?"

"You're pushing it."

She pursed her lips, and Crazy smiled. "No toy, you've got enough. Work your charms on Leanna. Let her know what an amazing dad I am."

"He'd get me a toy."

Pinching her nose, he tapped her bottom. "Get changed, and I'm going to go and make breakfast."

Getting to his feet, he made his way into the kitchen. Eggs and bacon were in the fridge, and he found some hash browns in the freezer.

He started cooking as his cell phone rang. Without looking who it was, he answered.

"Crazy."

"I need money."

Tensing, he stared down at his phone, and saw he didn't recognize the number.

"Fuck off, Suz. You've got to be fucking kidding me."

He was so angry that he almost smashed his phone. It was only the fact he'd smashed several phones in the last year that stopped him.

"I've got fucking nothing. You want me to keep my mouth shut, you'll fucking pay."

"Don't even think you can threaten me, whore."

"Strawberry's due at school this year. There's

nothing stopping me from going to the school, and taking my poor baby out of school."

"You've got a fucking death wish."

"I want money, and I don't care how I get it. Just get it to me."

The line disconnected. The rage built inside him, and he quickly dialed Duke. He was going to end Suz the moment he saw her. There was no way he was going to be blackmailed by a fucking slut every time she wanted some money.

"What?" Duke groaned.

"Are you cheating?"

"What? Fuck, no. Do you know what it's like to go camping on a blow up bed? Fuck me, I'm old. My back is fucking killing me."

Against all odds, Crazy laughed.

"Why did you call?" Duke asked, groaning some more.

"I just got a call off Suz."

"What does that slut want? Didn't she understand the warnings we gave her?"

Crazy sighed. *Apparently not.* "I'm not giving her any money. She needs to be dealt with. She threatened to take Strawberry away from me, and no one threatens to take my kid from me and gets away with it."

"Are you ready to take her life?"

"You took your ex's life."

"My ex almost killed Holly, and she was a bitch, and determined to fuck the club over. I didn't hesitate. You hesitated."

"I'm ready to kill her. I was ready to do so last time."

Duke sighed. "It's still not easy taking a life. I'll call Pike, and we'll handle this as a club matter."

"Let me know when you want church."

"Do you know where Suz is?"

"No. She'll come out of hiding for the money."

"Then we'll deal with her. Fucking way to start the weekend."

"See you soon, brother." Disconnecting the call, he leaned against the stove. He was so fucking angry. "Calm down." He got his name for going a little crazy when his anger got the better of him. He was so pissed off, and he didn't want to let Leanna see it. He'd never even directed it at Strawberry.

After several minutes of breathing in deeply, he finally gained control, and started to fry up some bacon.

Strawberry went to the sitting room, and he watched her turn the television on.

He really needed to get a home big enough. Strawberry deserved the chance to run out, play, and explore, not be stuck in front of the television. He didn't trust sending her outside on the patch of grass near the building. There were some sick fucks out there.

The bacon was sizzling, and the bread toasted, with the scrambled eggs keeping warm, when Leanna padded toward the kitchen. He saw she was wearing her jeans, and his shirt. She'd tucked her hair behind her ears, and she smiled at him.

Leanna looked so … pure. If she'd not come so hard on his fingers yesterday, he wouldn't believe it was the same woman staring back at him. She glanced toward Strawberry and took a seat.

"Did she wake up?"

"A few times. I promised I'd leave you to sleep, and I kept that promise."

"You didn't have to."

"She's my responsibility. I've got no problem with it. Besides, I liked watching you sleep."

She rolled her eyes.

"What do you have cooking there?"

"Breakfast."

He plated everything up, and called Strawberry to join them. It was a surreal experience, eating breakfast as a family. Crazy rarely sat down for breakfast.

Giving Strawberry the tap on the leg, he watched his little girl spring into action.

"You've got to come to dinner with us, Leanna. Daddy's going to buy ice cream, and me a toy."

The little minx.

"What?" Leanna asked, looking at him then at Strawberry.

"I promised Strawberry that I'd take her out for dinner, and ice cream. *If* she's good enough, she'll get a toy."

"It'll be fun," Strawberry said.

"It's her last summer before school."

He saw Leanna was caving.

"Sure. Why not?"

"Good."

Strawberry left to brush her teeth, and Crazy got to work on dinner.

"You put her up to that," Leanna said.

"What?" he asked, concentrating on the dishes in front of him. How the hell did she know that?

"I'm happy to go out to dinner with you, and with Strawberry. You didn't need to use her to manipulate me. Besides, she got a toy out of it."

"Can you believe I told her no to the toy, and yes to the ice cream?"

"I feel sorry for her teachers. If they're not careful, she's going to be running rings around them to get what she wants."

"I can't complain. She's my little girl."

Leanna chuckled, and he reached out, running his

thumb across her bottom lip.

"Tonight, I can't extend the invitation to spend the night."

"I don't expect you to be free." She bit her lip, and all he wanted to do was bite it. "You've got responsibilities, and I respect them. I adore Strawberry."

"How about Sunday night?"

"All of us together?"

"No, I can get one of the guys to babysit. I want to finish what we started last night."

"Damn twenty-four hour bugs."

He couldn't agree more.

Cupping her cheek, he tugged her close, and slammed his lips down on hers.

"Strawberry?" She spoke up in between kisses.

"It'll take her thirty minutes to do her teeth. I've got to kiss you."

Sliding his tongue into her mouth, he sank his fingers into her hair, and with his other hand, he glided his fingers beneath his shirt to touch her tits.

She was soft, and he moaned at the touch of her.

"I've got to go and get ready," she said.

"Okay. I'll collect you at three."

He kept hold of her hand, seeing her out of his apartment. Crazy didn't like watching her walk away. He needed to get her to stay with him, and he was willing to do whatever it took to speed it along.

She's not on the pill.

Crazy closed the door, and didn't like the way his thoughts were going. If he didn't get anywhere else with her, he could at least knock her up, and claim her like that. The very thought left a bitter taste in his mouth, but it was an option.

****

The dinner date turned out better than Leanna

thought it would. She enjoyed having fun, and even though they drew the attention of several customers, she still had fun. Crazy was attentive, and Strawberry was such a wonderful girl. For a few seconds she could pretend that the family was in fact hers. She'd always wanted a family, and had dreamed of one since she was little.

Leanna wanted a big family with several children. Failed relationships had made her squash that need for children, a man to love.

She'd left Crazy and Strawberry after dinner, going back to her own apartment to clean, and to just try to get her defenses back up. Nothing seemed to work though. Every time she thought about Crazy, she thought about the way his lips felt on her skin, on her pussy, and it made her want more from him.

When she finished cleaning her sitting room, and washing the covers on her couch, she got to work in her kitchen, then her bedroom. Once the entire apartment was clean, she sat down on the chair across from the couch, and stared at the spot that had weakened her against Crazy's touch.

Instead of building a guard around herself, she was weakening. Deciding against watching television, she went to bed early, only to wake up on Sunday more tired than the night before.

Binding her hair up on top of her head, she dressed in a pair of brown shorts and a crop top. It was getting hotter, and she turned the AC on to try to cool down.

She checked her mails, to find several updates waiting for her. There had been a successful takeover bid of a digital company, and a lot of other words that she didn't understand. This was why she'd never have made it in the corporate world. She had always wanted to be a small town wife and mother.

At around noon just as she was about to look at doing lunch, her doorbell rang.

Opening the door without looking who it was, she saw Crazy on the other side. There was a time when she would only ever see him every couple of days. Suz would bring Strawberry to the apartment, or not even bother to pick her up.

"So, I've been called, and asked to invite you."

She frowned looking from Strawberry up to Crazy. "To invite me to what?"

"To the barbeque. Holly called me. All the guys have gotten some meat, and are waiting for us. Would you like to join the Trojans for dinner?"

"Please, Leanna, please."

"I've got nothing better to do. Let me get changed."

"You're fine the way you are."

Glancing down at her shorts and top, she shook her head. "I'm not going to look a mess?"

"No. You'll fit right in, I can guarantee it."

Biting her lip, she touched her head, and couldn't believe how nervous she suddenly felt. The club women were all beautiful, sexy women. Leanna wasn't a sexy woman. She lacked in sexuality and all things feminine.

"Are you sure?"

Stepping close to her, he took her hand, running his thumb across her pulse. "You're perfect."

The way he stared at her left Leanna in no doubt that he spoke the truth. He wasn't trying to embarrass her.

Grabbing her keys, she followed him out.

"Daisy is picking us up."

She'd never get over a guy being named after a flower. It just didn't seem right to her, but then, she hadn't met the guy.

Walking outside she followed beside Crazy, and saw a minivan park up outside of them.

"Come on, suckers, time for us to eat."

She guessed that was Daisy. Helping Strawberry into the car seat, she moved around the side of the car, and as she reached for the door, Crazy stopped her, taking hold of her arm, and tugging her out of the way. He further surprised her when he opened the door, helping her inside the car. Crazy also strapped her in.

"I can do that," she said.

"I wanted to." He brushed his lips across her cheek, and for a split second the rest of the world fell away.

"Come on, lovebirds," Daisy said.

Crazy smiled, pulling away, and Leanna just wanted to hit Daisy. All morning she'd been thinking about Crazy's lips, and wanted them back on hers, ravishing her. Last night, her dreams had been filled with images of Crazy, and what he could do to her body.

Sitting back, she looked out of her window while listening to Daisy and Crazy talk about everything and nothing. Strawberry was playing with her doll, and Leanna went from watching the little girl, to looking out of the window, then back again.

"When's Beth and Maria coming in?"

"Later tonight or tomorrow morning."

"Are you sure you're happy to have Strawberry?"

"Are you kidding me? It'll give me a reason to stay out of my sister's way. She won't like being surrounded by her big brother."

"She staying at the club?"

"Yeah. Duke's got it all covered. The guys know her, and they know to keep their fucking hands to themselves. I caught the way Knuckles was looking at her picture, and I didn't fucking like it."

Crazy laughed. "Knuckles is probably fucking with you. You know he's on the darker side of everything."

"He can stay away from my sister."

Back and forth it went, and when she looked at Strawberry, the little girl looked happy about it. Leanna couldn't help but enjoy feeling like a family.

A sense of loneliness settled in the pit of her stomach, leaving her uncomfortable.

It wasn't long before they were pulling into the Trojans MC clubhouse. She'd never been to the clubhouse before, and had never wanted to. There were several motorbikes lined up in a row along one wall. The parking lot was large, and it held a mechanics shop off to the side, and she saw the shop was shut.

A couple of cars were parked, and the scent of barbeque was heavy in the air.

"They better not be grilling yet 'cause I had to come and get your ass," Daisy said.

Climbing out of the car, she followed behind Crazy. After a couple of steps, Crazy stopped, and took her hand.

"The guys won't bite."

Music played in the background, and when they rounded the building she watched as Strawberry squealed and rushed toward the play area for kids. She saw Matthew playing ball with a hoop on the side of the building. Most of the club members were dotted around the large backyard. There were several benches, and she saw Holly and Mary coming out, carrying trays of buns, which they put on several tables.

Mary let out a squeal as one guy tugged her down into his lap, kissing the side of her neck.

"That's Mary and Pike. They've been married a

year nearly, and have a baby girl."

She nodded, recognizing the couple.

"Come on, it's time to introduce you." He squeezed her hand a little tighter, as they made their way to one of the tables to where Holly had taken a seat.

Leanna recognized the little boy Drake sitting on a mean ass looking fucker. She had no doubt that he was the president of the MC. His reputation preceded him. He was so scary, and she didn't even know him.

"That's Duke holding his son Drake. It's confusing as fuck, but that's the way Holly wanted it."

"Hey, my boy came out a Drake. I couldn't help it," Holly said, pressing a sloppy kiss to her boy's face.

"That's Russ and Sheila. Russ used to be the president of this place before he handed it over to Duke."

"Nice to meet you," she said.

"It would be nice to get the woman's name," Russ said.

"This is Leanna."

She reached out taking each of their hands in turn. "It's nice to meet you."

"You're one of those good girls aren't you?" Russ said, eyeing her up and down.

"I, erm, I don't know if I would be considered a good girl, but I do my best."

Russ chuckled. "Yep, this girl is a keeper, Crazy. It's about time you found a woman worth your time."

Wow, she couldn't believe that they would say that to Crazy, and when she glanced behind her, Crazy was already smiling.

"She really is."

He wrapped his hand around her waist and started to stroke her hip. She was a little unnerved about him touching her because she didn't have a smooth stomach or tight muscles. Leanna had already spotted the table with the sweet-butts on it. They were the only women sitting at the table, and they were eyeing some of the men. Also, none of them had a guy around them, laying claim. Holly had Duke who was constantly touching her. Mary and Pike were all over each other, and Russ held the back of Sheila's neck.

There were several other couples, but Crazy took a seat at the table with Russ and Duke.

"That grill is ready to be used, baby," Holly said.

"Go and get me some meat, and I'll start grilling."

"Can I help?" Leanna asked. She hated not being able to do something, and sitting with a load of men while Holly went off to work, didn't sit well with her.

"Sure. Come on. Mary, stop getting your ass felt up, and come and help me."

"See, you got me told off," Mary said, slapping Pike on the shoulder.

"Baby, your ass got you in trouble not me. You know I can't resist that ass." He pinched her flesh once again, and Leanna's cheeks flamed at the open lust Pike was showing.

Walking into the kitchen of the clubhouse, Leanna fell in love. She saw instantly that this was the kitchen for all of the women. "It's a dream, isn't it?" Holly asked. "Duke and the men love their food, and I'm more than happy to provide it."

"We've got our own food blog going on, and it's so good," Mary said.

"You both seem happy."

"We are. I mean, how could we not? Our men love us. With the Trojans, we're protected, and we're like one big happy family." This came from Mary.

"Raoul's getting hungry, and Landon is pissing him off." A woman with red hair came into the kitchen.

All three women were wearing summer dresses that came to their knees. She noticed none of them were overly dressed, or under dressed for the occasion.

"Aren't any of you concerned about those women—" She cut off her thoughts, and stayed silent. "I'm sorry. This is none of my business."

"The sweet-butts, or the club whores, are for the men who are not married, and want an easy fuck," Holly said. "I'm not going to lie, they piss me off sometimes. They think they're entitled because they're here, but they are in no way club property the way we are."

"What do you mean?" Leanna asked, turning her attention from the women, who were trying to gain attention from several of the club members.

"Old ladies, like myself, Mary, and Zoe, we belong to one of the members, so we get the respect from the men. We're protected, and no one else will touch us."

"If you're one of those women, there is no one man. Whoever wants you, takes you, and you've got to accept that. No man will call you an old lady, and no man will fight with a club member over them. They're like living, breathing, blow up dolls. They are protected from outsiders, but that is it."

Leanna didn't know if she liked what she had just learned, but at least Crazy had never called her a club whore.

Maybe there was hope for them yet.

Chapter Six

"She's a keeper, Crazy," Russ said.

"You shouldn't be leading her on to be a mother for Strawberry. It's not fair on her," Sheila said.

"I'm not using her. Believe it or not, I actually like her." Crazy did like her. She was unlike any of the other women he'd been with, and glancing over at the club whores, he knew she wasn't like them.

He didn't want any of those sluts talking to Leanna. Whatever they had to say was to be kept to themselves.

"They know to keep their mouths shut right?"

"Yes," Duke said. "I talked to them, and they know how to stay silent. They want to remain in the club then they stay silent, or they are gone. No second chances."

Duke was angry with the club whores, especially with Suz, trying to influence them. Since Duke had married Holly, he didn't even bother touching the club whores, so he was tired of them constantly causing trouble.

"Speaking of second chances, what do we do to deal with Suz?" Russ asked. "Duke let me know that she's demanding more money or threatening to take Strawberry when she starts school."

"Is this my cue to leave?" Sheila asked.

Russ took her hand. "No, babe. You need to be here."

"I told you Suz would be a problem when she came to the clubhouse, and she's proven that."

Suz had been a club whore back when Russ was the president of the club.

"I know, and I'm sorry."

Sheila shook her head. "There's not a lot you can do about it. She's clearly got a death wish, or she really does think she has a chance of getting what she wants."

"She's just a bitch that is pushing her luck. Suz doesn't have a hold on this club, so she's going for my kid. I wouldn't have her near my girl."

"What does Leanna know about her?" Duke asked.

"That Suz left because she knows what is good for her. It's not a lie." Crazy ran a hand down his face.

"We talking about Suz?" Daisy asked, taking a seat. "Just so you know, the girls are letting your girl know the difference between a whore and an old lady."

Crazy cursed.

"Relax. Holly knows not to tell her anything about the claiming. My old lady won't spill the details."

Crazy wasn't ready for Leanna to know how the guys claimed their woman in front of the club. The only woman he'd ever seen happy about being taken was Zoe with Raoul. Club whores were initiated into the club by being taken by several men, shared around, and that was how they got their place within the club. For an old lady, the club member had sex with her in front of the club, but no one was allowed to touch. The men accepted her as being that person's property, so for Crazy, Leanna would belong to him, and no other man would touch her.

He liked the thought of no one else touching her.

Holly, Mary, Zoe, and Leanna all came out carrying trays of food.

"That's my turn. I hope you're all hungry." Duke got to his feet, taking the trays from Holly, and giving her a kiss.

The other three women stayed in line for Duke to start putting the burgers, and steaks onto the grill.

Crazy took the time to simply watch her. Leanna

was a beautiful woman, and her beauty wasn't covered or enhanced with makeup. Her hair was piled on her head, and the clothes she wore molded to her body like a second skin. She looked … innocent. He intended to mess with all that innocence, and make her a little bit dirty.

Dirty would look really good on her.

His cock started to swell, and he shifted in his seat. Holly came out, arranging the main table with salads, buns, and many other assortments that were needed for a barbeque.

"I can't cook," Zoe said, taking a seat beside Raoul.

"I know, baby. It's why we're going to spend all of our days here."

She slapped his chest, and Crazy chuckled.

"How are you for a cook, Leanna?" Russ asked.

Crazy took his woman's hand, and tugged her down beside him.

"I, erm, I think I cook okay. Strawberry's never complained."

"And neither have I." Crazy pushed some hair off her shoulder, and pressed his nose against her neck. She smelled so good, and like home.

Conversation started up, and Crazy was happy it wasn't about sex, or the club whores. They were talking about Mac, the guy who owned the diner that Mary was part owner of.

"We've got that festival in town in a couple of weeks," Russ said.

"I always take my lasagna to the event," Leanna said.

"Lasagna?"

"Yes, I tend to make three pots of the stuff."

The men were looking at her, and Sheila licked

her lips.

"What's up?" Leanna asked.

"How is your lasagna made?" Crazy asked.

Every year without fail, he always went to the potluck festival in Vale Valley. It was a town event that had everyone in the center of town, and they were surrounded by different dishes that were made by townsfolk. It was a huge success, and every year he always charged forward to taste, to him, the best lasagna in the world. It was layers of tomato, cheese, white sauce, and lasagna sheets. It was the best thing he'd ever tasted.

"Well, it starts with a layer of cheese sauce, then white sauce, and I mound the meat sauce over cooked lasagna sheets. I then repeat the layers until all of the trays I use are full." Leanna's cheeks were heating. "I haven't given anyone food poisoning, have I?"

"No, you've not," Crazy said.

"Fuck me, you were the one that has the heavenly lasagna," Raoul said.

"Raoul's told me about that," Zoe said. "I've never seen him look so happy about food before."

"You've never made me lasagna," Crazy said.

"I have for Strawberry."

He was jealous of his daughter.

Suddenly, everyone started talking to her, asking for her to make it for a Sunday gathering.

The club was vying for her attention, and once Mary and Holly heard, they were around.

"Have you ever seen our food blog?" Mary asked.

It wasn't long before a laptop came out, and Leanna was pulled away, looking at some of the food.

Once the food was out, Crazy was hoping to get Leanna back to him, but it didn't work. Mary got them three burgers, and the three women sat around, eating.

"Your girl fits right in," Russ said.

"Yeah, she does."

"I'd be careful. Holly and Mary can talk food all the time," Duke said.

Crazy watched as Pike moved up behind his woman, kissing her neck. Mary's eyes closed, and she leaned back.

That was what he wanted with Leanna, to be able to touch her, and her melt against him.

What was wrong with wanting something like that?

"What the fuck are you doing here?" Daisy said, suddenly interrupting the steady flow of conversation. He sounded pissed, and was glaring toward the entrance of the garden. Turning around, he saw Beth, his sister, and a woman with incredibly dark raven hair.

"Is that anyway to speak to me? I've been trying to call you, and you wouldn't answer," Beth said, holding up her phone. "Some big brother you are."

"You said you wouldn't be here tonight, or tomorrow."

"No, I didn't. In the message I said I'd be here *today*. Seriously, don't you ever listen?" Beth was smiling as she talked.

Crazy had met Beth a few times when she came to visit, which wasn't often. The young girl had grown up, and he saw a maturity in her eyes that only came from a broken heart.

"Hey, Daisy," Beth said.

Daisy walked over, pulling her in for a hug. "Damn, I'm sorry. I really thought you weren't coming until tomorrow. If I'd known, I would have been there to pick you up."

"It's okay. We took a cab, and there was one who was happy to drop us off at the Trojans' clubhouse."

Beth looked toward the group, and smiled. "Hey, everyone."

They all nodded their hello to Beth. She wasn't an old lady, but she was part of the family.

"This is Maria. She's my friend, and will be with us."

Maria held her hand up, waving. She held a bag tightly to her.

"Come on, we won't bite. I'll get you settled in. Shit," Daisy said, looking toward him. "I can't take care of Strawberry tonight."

"It's okay," Crazy asked, disappointed that he would have to go another night of not getting in Leanna's pants, which only served to piss him off. He wasn't happy about that, not in the slightest.

He didn't want to think about his dick right now, but he'd been let down.

"We'll take her," Russ said.

Sheila nodded. "We've got Holly's little one, Matthew, and Mary's girl. We're happy to take Strawberry as well."

"Alone time is called for everyone." Russ gave him a wink, and when Crazy looked toward the small group of women, he saw each of them was wearing red faces.

Chuckling, he waved Strawberry over, and made sure his daughter was happy with that.

Of course, she was so damn happy about it, and again Crazy felt guilty for keeping his little girl away from the club, his family.

It was all going to change. He was going to make sure of it.

****

Later that night after all the kids had disappeared, the beer came out, and the music was turned up. Lights hung around the back of the clubhouse, and it really looked beautiful. The club whores started to mingle with the other members, and Leanna was … happy. Leaning against Crazy, she sighed at the pleasure of him stroking her thigh.

"It was nice of Russ and Sheila," she said.

"They always wanted more kids but couldn't have them."

Crazy pulled hair off her shoulder, and started to kiss and suck on her neck. Closing her eyes, she loved the feel of his lips on her neck. One of his hands rested below her breast, and he kept touching her, which only served to heighten her need for him.

"Did you enjoy yourself today?"

"Yes. I like Holly and Mary."

Both women had disappeared, following behind their husbands. Leanna's pussy clenched as Crazy pressed against her ass. "Do you feel what you do to me?"

"Yes. Will we be interrupted tonight?" she asked.

"No. Sheila and Russ know what to do. Strawberry had a twenty-four hour bug. She's more than fine." Crazy kissed her neck. "Do you want me to show you my room?"

"What will happen if I go to your room?" she asked.

"It's quite simple, but I'll tell you anyway. You come to my room, I'm going to lock the door, get you naked, and bend you over my bed. I'll remove my clothes, and spread the cheeks of your ass wide so I can stare at your ass and pussy."

She took a deep breath, watching the glow of the twinkling lights around her.

"When I've got you nice and wet, I'm going to slide my dick so deep inside you, you're screaming, and begging me for more, and not to stop. If you don't want that, then tell me. I'll take you home."

"I don't want to go home."

No, she wanted the pleasure that only Crazy could give her. He'd been driving her crazy for the past couple of years, but he didn't know that. She'd wanted him a long time, and now she was going to finally have him.

"Come on."

He pressed another kiss to her neck and got to his feet. She placed her hand into his, and they left the backyard. No one said anything, and her face was on fire at what they must be thinking.

"You want this, Leanna."

This was the most adventure she'd ever experienced in her life. They passed one room, and Leanna gasped. Inside, she saw one of the women, dancing around the pole, going up and down it, and she was naked.

"I hope she cleans that," Leanna said, having stopped to watch.

Crazy stood behind her, running his hand down to cup her pussy.

The woman on the pole was pressed tight against it, and Leanna saw her bare pussy was massaging the pole as if it was a cock.

It made her feel a little unnerved. This was the kind of sensuality and raw sex that he was around all the time. She couldn't compete with that.

"You're not here, and I don't ever expect you to be a club whore, Leanna. I don't want her. I want you."

He pressed his dick against her ass, and she glanced behind her to see Crazy was looking at her, and not another woman. "Come with me."

She didn't look back, and followed Crazy up

several flights of stairs. They stopped at the first room on the second floor.

Crazy pulled out a key and unlocked the door. "I keep it locked so no one will come in, and steal my shit. Actually, that's wrong. I locked my door because Suz would steal my shit. I'm not interested in my stuff being messed with, and I never trusted Suz."

He closed and locked the door once they'd stepped inside.

Turning to face him, she saw Crazy was leaning against the door, blocking her escape, not that she intended to escape.

"Take your clothes off."

Raising a brow, Leanna pressed a hand to her stomach.

"When we're in your place, I'll take it slow. We're in my room at the clubhouse. This is my domain, and I'm not going to hold back who I am, Leanna, not from you, not from anyone."

"I don't expect you to hold anything back from me."

"Then accept that I'm the one that will always be in charge. I need to be in charge no matter what."

Biting her lip, she saw the truth in his eyes. "You're the one in charge?"

"Yes. I'm a dominant man."

"Like whips and chains?"

"No. Not like that. I don't need to use whips to get off. I simply need a woman who has no fear, and is more than prepared to trust me with her body, and with her pleasure. Do you trust me not to hurt you, Leanna?"

Licking her lips again, Leanna tilted her head to the side, unsure of how to answer.

He wants trust.

He wants you to give into him, to submit.

The thought didn't repulse her. She wanted to be with him, to give him everything that he wanted.

"Yes, I do." Crazy had never hurt her, never given her reason to doubt his sincerity.

"Then take off your clothes, and do it quickly. I don't like to be kept waiting."

Keeping her gaze on his, she kicked her sneakers off, then worked her shorts down. When she couldn't keep eye contact, she started tugged off her shirt, until she stood before him in her underwear.

"Did I say you could keep anything on? Lose the panties and bra."

Taking a deep, shuddering breath, she removed her bra and panties. Standing before him naked, Leanna didn't know what else to do, so she stood a few feet away from him, and waited.

"Look at me, Leanna."

Another deep breath, and she looked up at him.

The moment her eyes caught his, she was lost. He removed his jacket, and stepped away from the door. "I don't play games. You want to leave, then tell me to stop. I'll listen to you."

Next came his shirt, followed by his jeans. His cock sprang forward, and Leanna wanted to taste him. She wanted to know what it felt like to have his dick sliding across her tongue to the back of her throat.

Sinking to her knees, she saw that she surprised him.

Wrapping her fingers around his length, she started to work the length, watching the tip leak pre-cum.

Pushing away all of her doubts, she flicked her tongue over the tip, and moaned at the taste of his pre-cum. He was salty, and she wanted more. She wanted to suck him until he came on her tongue.

"Fuck, baby, you've got a dirty side to you, and I

fucking love it." He sank his fingers in her hair, and she didn't pull away from him. She loved it when he touched her, took control. The men she'd been with hadn't wanted to take control. This was what made him so different, and she didn't want it to end.

He removed the band in her hair so that the length fell around her shoulders, and he gathered the length in his grip, wrapping it around his wrist, and holding onto her tightly.

She took the whole tip into her mouth, moaning as he filled her.

Crazy wasn't a small man. He was large, and she opened her mouth wider to accommodate him.

"Your mouth is perfect, Leanna."

Leanna took him deep until he hit the back of her throat, and she pulled away, gasping, only to tease his balls, cupping them in her palm.

With her other hand, she covered his saliva covered cock, and started to work up and down.

"Yes, that's it. Fuck, your lips are so good."

Glancing up, she saw he was staring down at her, watching her.

"Use your teeth, lightly graze up my length."

She did what he asked, and he closed his eyes, bowing his head back.

He gripped the back of her head, thrusting his cock in deep, and she took it, moaning. "Yes, suck my cock."

Removing her hand, she kept her jaw slack, and took him.

"I'm going to come. Do you want me to pull out?"

She'd never swallowed a man's cum before, and she didn't know if she wanted to.

Do it.

Leanna wanted to give Crazy everything, so she closed her eyes, and moaned. Reaching between her thighs, she stroked her clit.

"You're touching yourself, aren't you? There's a dirty little bitch inside you begging to get out. Don't worry, Leanna, I'll take care of her, and she can come out with me. There's no way I'm sharing you. You're a treasure I'm going to keep to myself."

She wasn't insulted.

He spoke the truth. She'd always dampened down her need as the men always seemed a little put off by what she wanted.

"I'm close, baby."

Pulling off his cock so that only the tip of him was inside her mouth, Leanna waited, sucking hard on the tip.

Crazy's dick jerked, and suddenly her mouth was filled with his warm, salty cum. Staring into his eyes, she felt his hand go around her neck. "Swallow it."

She did as he ordered, and Crazy groaned, feeling her neck, as she swallowed down his cum.

The moment she'd milked him dry, he pulled out of her mouth, grabbed her arms, and forced her up. Within seconds, she was on the bed, and he had her legs open.

Leanna looked down to see him spread the lips of her pussy open, and flick his tongue across her wet pussy.

"You're already soaking wet, Leanna."

"I want you."

"You want my tongue?"

"Yes."

"Do you want my dick?"

"I want whatever you want to give me. Please, Crazy."

He slid a finger inside her pussy, curling it around until he was stroking over her G-spot.

"Don't ever hold back from me, Leanna. You want to fuck me, then you come to me, call me, text me, you name it—I want to know. I want to know if you want to be made love to, or bent over a desk, couch, bed, and fucked until you can't remember your name." The finger inside her pulled out, and slid down to the crack of her ass. She gasped, tightening up without meaning to. "You ever had a dick here?"

"No!"

"You will. I'll fuck your ass, and have you begging for more."

Before she could refute his claim, Crazy sucked her clit into his mouth, and she couldn't think. He pressed against her ass, and it fought against the odd penetration. Crazy wouldn't let up.

"Push out."

Following his instruction, she pushed out, and the tip of his finger pushed forward, going past her anus. There was pain and pleasure combined.

"You're incredibly tight. I'm going to take this ass, claim it for my own, baby."

She whimpered but couldn't deny it. Her body was no longer her own, but the property of Crazy.

Chapter Seven

Daisy knocked on his sister's door. There was a small part of the clubhouse that was for family members only, and it had been a couple of years since his sister had visited. The last time had to have been when she was fourteen, with his mother. The club had kept their sexual needs private while his family visited.

Beth opened the door and smiled up at him. "Hey, big brother."

"I'm just making sure you've settled in okay."

"I have. Maria is across the hall. Thank you so much for putting up with us."

"Mom said you needed to get away for the summer. What is going on?" Daisy asked, folding his hands across his chest.

Beth tucked some hair behind her ear, and looked at the floor. "It's, erm, it's personal, and I really don't want my scary big brother knowing about it."

"Why?"

"Look, let's just say something happened, and you'd go and kick someone's ass. I don't want you to do that. I want to get away from everything, and just stay here."

Daisy sighed. "I'll find out."

"I really hope not." She went onto her toes, and kissed his cheek. "I love you, Daisy, but this isn't something you can change with your fists."

"Everything can be handled with violence."

Beth shook her head. "You don't think that. You can't think that. Behind all that hard ass, you're still my big brother."

"Big brothers grow up, and realize that to get what you want, you got to be prepared to hurt others."

His sister winced. "We'll talk more in the morning."

"Good night, Beth." He kissed her head and watched as she turned away, closing the door.

"Don't push her."

He spun to find Maria leaning up against her doorframe. She'd been quiet, and he hadn't even heard her move.

"I'll find out who hurt her."

Maria's expression went blank, and she took a step back into her room.

Daisy didn't want their interaction to end, so he stepped into her room and closed the door behind him.

Her arms were folded across her chest. She hadn't changed out of her summer dress, but she had let her hair down. The black length fell across her body in waves. Was her hair as silky as it looked? No one could be that perfect. He refused to believe it.

"What do you want, Daisy?" Maria asked.

"You've all grown up."

She chuckled. "Like you said, big brothers grow up, and so do best friends. I grew up." She held her hands out before dropping them to her side.

"You certainly did." He couldn't help but admire the curves of her body. Her tits were nice and large, straining to get out of the top of her dress.

"You're being crude. My face is up here." She waved her hand in front of her chest, and tutted. "You're typical, you know that. You're just like every other man."

"What happened with Beth?"

"None of your business. All you can do is help her by giving her a fun summer."

"I could do that without you. Why did you come along?"

"I'm her best friend, and her mother didn't want her to come alone. I'm here to make sure she has a good time."

"You know, women go to the beach, or away to another country for the summer."

"Then it should give you a clue that Beth is hurting so much, and is so frightened that she ran to her big brother, who happens to be part of a powerful MC."

Daisy tensed up. "What the fuck are you saying?"

Maria licked her lips and took a seat on the bed.

"I'm saying that Beth's here because she feels protected by you. She told me she didn't want to go to Ibiza or Spain or Italy to get away. She wanted to come here where her big brother would keep every man away."

"I will find out what is going on."

"Good luck. You won't get it out of me."

Daisy took a step toward her. "I've got many ways of getting what I want out of women."

"You mean sluts?" Maria asked, standing up. "Go ahead, Daisy. I'm not one of the women who want to impress you. I'm your sister's best friend. I'm off limits. You said so yourself. I got over my crush."

"You heard me wrong, Maria." He sank his fingers into her hair, and he got his answer. Her hair was silky to the touch. "I didn't say you were off limits because of my sister. I said you were off limits because you're the same age as my sister. Last time I checked, you're old enough to fuck without me being thrown in jail for statutory rape. You're old enough, and I guess we can put your lack of a crush to the test." He trailed his other finger down the curve of her neck, breathing over her pulse, which was pounding rapidly. "I think you're lying, Maria. You want me, and I bet your pussy is wet for me."

Maria brought her knee up, slamming it against

his balls. Releasing her, Daisy cupped his dick, and wondered if he was ever going to father children. She'd caught him completely off guard.

"You're wrong. I don't want you. I've never wanted you. You're used goods, Daisy. I'm better than that."

She opened her door, and he stumbled out.

"This isn't over."

"It was over a long time ago, Daisy."

The door slammed, and he winced.

Well, the young woman had grown claws. Maria had put up a wall around her, but he was more than ready to tear down whatever wall she thought she could have. Maria was going to be his.

Chapter Eight

Crazy pumped his finger into her ass and added a second one. Leanna's cream leaked out of her pussy, and he swallowed it down. The cum that got to her ass, he began to work into her, lubricating his finger.

"That's it, baby." He added a second finger into her ass, and bit down on her nipple, creating a small bite of pain.

Leanna arched up, pressing her pussy against his face, and he moved his tongue down to her pussy, sliding his cock into her hole.

"Yes, yes, Crazy, it feels so good."

Using his thumb he slid in and out of her, taking his time, and fucking her pussy.

Sliding his tongue over her clit, he brought her closer and closer to orgasm. Keeping her at the peak of pleasure, he waited until she was begging him before he caved, and gave in to her. Leanna screamed out his name, begging for more. Her pussy thrust up against his mouth, and he pushed his fingers into her ass. She became more open, and he took full advantage.

Only when she couldn't stand it anymore, did she start to pull away, pleading with him to stop.

Crazy pressed a final kiss to her pussy and removed his fingers from her ass. "I'll be right back." He washed his fingers in the sink, and brought back a damp cloth. Leanna was lying on her side, and when she saw him, she sat up.

"It's okay. Lie down."

She went back to lying down. He opened her thighs and pressed the damp cloth between them, cleaning away the access cream.

"Wow," she said. Leanna covered her face with

her hand, and he chuckled.

"Don't go hiding yourself from me."

"I can't believe that just happened."

"You better believe it. I'm not done with you tonight." He threw the cloth toward the bathroom and placed his hand on her rounded stomach. "I figured you would be comfortable if I removed the evidence of your need for me."

Sliding his hand up her body, he circled the nipple that was farther away from him. Pinching the bud, he heard her gasp, and her tits shuddered as she took a deep breath.

"Why don't you work?" he asked.

He'd done a thorough background search on her, only to discover that she didn't actually have an occupation but she was a wealthy woman.

"What?"

"You heard me." He released her breast, and rested his palm on her stomach. "Tell me."

She licked her lips, and he remembered the way they felt wrapped around his dick. "I, er, it's complicated. I thought we were here for sex?"

He shook his head. "We're going to learn to talk to each other. I have stakes in the club, and the money we earn from the mechanic shop and the stock markets are split equally among us all." He didn't mention some of the runs the club did. She didn't need to know about them, and they were growing even less frequent. "You know about Suz, and my kid. Tell me something about you."

Leanna stared at him for several seconds.

"Okay, you want to talk."

She sat up, and he wouldn't let her hide. Grabbing her foot, he wrapped his fingers around her ankle, and tugged her back down to the bed. Moving between her thighs, he grabbed her hands, and placed them above her head.

"Let's talk like this."

Leanna opened up a lot more when he invaded her space, and that was exactly what he was doing now, invading her very private space.

His cock stirred to life, and he wanted to fuck her again. Instead, he made sure his mind was on her words.

"I can talk to you without you being this close."

"Nah, I don't think so. Talk."

"How do you know I don't work?"

"Let's say, I did a background check on you. You're not even registered as an employee in town, or out of town."

She clicked her tongue, and sighed. "I don't need to work. One of the problems I had with my ex-husband is that he knew I was wealthy."

"You're wealthy?"

"Yes, very wealthy, and with money comes a lot of problems. I don't handle the company in any way. I'm just given money, and regular updates. My grandparents made sure I was more than taken care of. The same will happen when or if I have kids. If I die, my grandfather has made sure that the company gets split down, and sold."

"What was this about your ex?" Crazy asked.

"I've just told you I'm a wealthy woman, and you're more interested in my ex?"

"I don't give a fuck about your money, Leanna. I want you, and your body. Money doesn't come into it. I've got my own. Now, your ex."

"He found out that I was a wealthy woman, and used me to get his ass through college. Do you know, I was so in love with him that I didn't want him to find out about the money, so I worked three jobs to support his ass?"

"Why not dig into your money? Go to college yourself?"

"I didn't want him to know about it. I was brought up to respect money, not to make it something it wasn't."

"So, this guy couldn't have been that important."

"How do you figure?"

"If you're in love with someone, you don't keep anything back. You're open and honest with the man or woman you love."

"You're open and honest?"

"Not with Suz, but then I never claimed to be in love with her. You, however, I've never lied to. I've always been honest."

She took a breath, and he saw the confusion in her eyes.

"I don't believe you're in love with me."

He tilted his head to the side, and stared down at her mouth. "That's fine, but I can tell you something, I very well could be."

His cock was rock hard as her soft body wriggled underneath him.

Slamming his lips down on hers, he plundered her mouth with his tongue, and she moaned against him. She wrapped her legs around his waist, and he growled out, wanting to be deep inside her.

Releasing one of her hands, he reached between them, grabbing his rock hard cock, and finding her entrance. He pushed the tip inside, and already she was fucking beautiful, and tight.

Pulling away from the kiss, he stared into her eyes, and slammed every inch of his dick into her cunt. She was so tight that he knew it had been a long time since she'd been with a man. He was going to get her used to the feel of his dick. Every time she moved, she was going to think about how hard and thick he was.

"You're so tight, and perfect."

He glided out of her slick pussy, and saw his dick covered in her cum. Leanna looked between them, and started to push him.

"What's the matter?" he asked.

"You're in me without a condom. Get a condom. I'm not protected."

"We can handle whatever is thrown at us, baby."

She shook her head. "No, that's not going to happen. You've got Strawberry, and whatever happens between us, it's not going to be because I'm pregnant. I've been married once for what they can get out of me. I'm not going to be forced into a second marriage because of a kid."

He growled out. "I wouldn't care."

"I care. I want to fuck you, Crazy, but until I get on some form of contraception, you're going to have to accept the fact I don't want to get pregnant. I'm not ready."

Pressing his head to her, he groaned. She had a point, and he didn't want to be compared to the assholes who'd used her.

You were going to use her.

He was going to use her, but he wasn't anymore.

Crazy was determined to be different, and to find a place within her heart.

Pulling out of her tight cunt, he reached for his nightstand, and opened up the drawer, begging that he had condoms inside. He gave a quick cheer when he saw there were at least three. Tomorrow he was going to go and buy out the supply at the pharmacy.

Rearing back on the bed, he tore into the foil, removing the latex. Aligning the tip, he rolled down the condom until he was secure.

"Thank you," Leanna said.

"Your wish is my command. Now, I can do this." Placing the tip at her core, he slammed inside her without giving her the chance to grow accustomed to his length. He didn't rest either. He pounded inside her, going to the hilt.

Gripping her hips, he tugged her back onto his cock as he pounded forward. He didn't stop, needing to make his mark inside her.

"You feel that, baby? You feel how deep I am inside you? It doesn't matter if I wear a rubber or not. I'm always going to be inside you."

"Yes."

"I'm going to fuck you raw until you forget everything else, and all that remains is us."

Crazy had never felt this possessive over the women he fucked. He wanted to own every part of Leanna, and for her to not look at another man, and to only ever look at him. It was consuming, scary as shit, but something he wasn't going to stop.

He pulled out of her pussy, opening her thighs, and staring down at her cunt, which was open from his cock. Slipping his fingers inside her pussy, he groaned. "You're so fucking hot for me. If you could see that pussy, you'd know what I wanted, and this was about a lot more than fucking."

"Crazy?"

"I can wait."

Flipping her over, he ran his hands over her ass. "I can wait for a long time, and while I wait, I'm going to fuck you until you become addicted to my cock."

****

Leanna screamed out as he plundered inside her pussy. He wasn't a small man, and he filled her to the top, and stretched her in ways she'd never been used before. Gripping the sheets, she tried to hold on while the pleasure he worked over her body was taking her breath away. He slapped her ass, gripped her hips, and slammed inside her. The sounds filling the room were those of flesh hitting flesh. She cried out he touched her clit, coating his fingers.

"You've got no idea how fucking hot you look. I want to fuck that sweet little ass of yours, but I can't. I've got to give you time. I'm going to play with you, Leanna."

The fingers on her clit disappeared, and she moaned as those same slick fingers started to tease her ass. It was too much, and yet she fucked back against his cock.

His other hand traced up her back, and tightened her hair in his fist, pulling her back. She was lifted up and Crazy held every part of her.

"Look at yourself in the mirror, Leanna. Look at the woman I'm fucking right now."

He turned her head, and Leanna gasped. When she entered the room, she hadn't taken into account the mirrors decorating the walls on the far side of the bed. Crazy looked dominating as he held her in position, plowing his dick inside her. She watched his cock appear, and disappear inside her.

"When you're on the pill, I'm going to fuck you until I spunk inside you, and then I'm going to watch my seed spill out of your pussy. I can't fucking wait. I'm going to fuck you everywhere, so no one else will have a chance to touch you. I'll own you, Leanna."

She couldn't look away from the sight of them. He was touching her ass, held her hair in place, and fucking her all at the same time. The pleasure intensified, and she reached down between her thighs, and started to stroke her clit.

"So fucking sexy. I knew you had it in you. One night was never going to be enough with you."

Moaning, Leanna stroked down until she felt his cock sliding in and out of her.

"Fuck, yes, touch us fucking. We're fucking one, baby."

Crying out, Leanna came as Crazy continued to pound inside her, and she gasped, moaning, and coming all together.

"Yes."

Crazy lost control and started to fuck her harder, making her take the whole length of his dick. She couldn't deny him, didn't want to deny him, and slammed back against him, wanting him to be as deep as he could.

"Yes, yes, yes," she said, chanting.

"Fuck!" Crazy slammed inside her one final time and even with the condom separating them, she felt the pulse of his cock as he filled the condom.

When it was over, they collapsed together on the bed, panting. He released her hair, and Leanna turned her head. "Why do you have a mirror opposite your bed?" she asked.

Crazy chuckled, pulling out of her ass and pussy. She watched as he removed the condom, tying it up, and throwing it in the trash.

"Why do you think?"

"You like to watch."

He stood at the end of the bed, and she watched him caress her body. "I like to watch. I like to see what I'm doing."

Leanna moaned as he slid his fingers into her pussy, pumping them in and out.

"What about the whole 'coming in me'?" she

asked.

Crazy chuckled. "I want to fuck you without a condom." He urged her up the bed, and he lay down beside her. She pushed some hair off her face, and watched as he turned to face her, his hand running up and down her arm, creating goosebumps on her flesh. "It's what turns me on. I don't know why, but I want to push my cum inside you, and when I've filled your tight little cunt with all of my cum, I want to watch it spill out."

She couldn't help but be aroused, and she shouldn't. That was the kind of stuff porn stars did, not her.

"I see you're struggling."

"That's for porn," she said, speaking her thoughts.

"When we're here together, we can do whatever we want. I won't judge you, and I don't want you to judge me." He moved his hand down, and started working his finger between her thighs. "This here, it tells me you're not as disgusted by what I want as you make out."

"I know."

"You're going to have to get used to it, baby. I'm not going to pretend with you. Would you like me to pretend, make love to you vanilla style, and find another pussy to satisfy my craving?"

"No. I don't want you to do that."

"Then we experiment. We have fun, and you learn not to hide from me."

She nodded and stared at his chest.

"Open up to me, Leanna."

"I will."

"You like the feel of my dick inside your pussy?"

"Yes."

"Are you going to get on the pill?"

"Yes."

"Are you getting on the pill so I can fuck your pussy, and watch my cum spill out of your lips?"

She licked her lips and forced herself to stare back at him. "Yes."

"Good."

He leaned forward, and pressed his lips to hers.

"Do we have to leave?" she asked.

"No. We've got all night, and I intend to use the last of my condoms, and have you screaming my name."

She was pushed back to the bed, and Leanna moaned as he pressed her tits together. He took one nipple, and she didn't put up a fight. There was no need to fight with what he wanted. She wanted it just as much, and it wasn't just about want—it was more about need.

Chapter Nine

One week later Crazy stared around the house that was near a street away from Mary and Pike's. He'd been looking for a place for some time, and nothing had caught his attention. Moving from the sitting room, into the dining room, then into the kitchen, Crazy knocked on the counter while trying to think.

The realtor was giving him a wide berth, which he didn't mind. He didn't want the little shit anywhere near him when he was trying to make a decision.

"Why didn't you bring Leanna?" Daisy asked coming into the kitchen. "Why bring us?"

Knuckles came into the kitchen from the playroom, and Crazy stared down at the floor plan in his hand.

"She's busy, and I didn't want to drag Strawberry around looking at houses," Crazy said.

"But you're more than happy to drag us around?" Knuckles asked, rounding the kitchen island. "It's a pretty decent home."

"Open the door to the garden," Crazy said, pointing at the door then at the realtor.

"Yes, sir." The kid was practically shitting himself at having three bikers in the same house. The keys rattled from the shaking, and Knuckles snorted. "I wonder how he'd cope with the club full coming to visit."

"What?" the realtor asked with a high pitched voice.

"Nothing."

Crazy stepped out into the large back yard. There was a patio area that was ready for a barbeque, along with several chairs.

"I don't want to give Leanna a reason to run. I refuse to let that happen, so I want to make sure I can make this decision on my own."

"Are you going to be claiming her as your old lady?" Knuckles asked.

"Yes."

"It has been a week," Daisy said. "How the fuck you know she's the one?"

Looking over at Daisy, he saw his brother was struggling with Beth and her friend being at the club.

"It has been longer than a week, and I know what I want, and I want Leanna."

For the past week he'd used any excuse he could to be with her. He'd even convinced her to be with him while Strawberry slept. After nearly getting caught by his daughter on Tuesday evening, he'd gone to the local DIY store, and found a bedroom lock.

It had been a week of adventure, and he just couldn't believe how much he enjoyed spending time with Leanna. He'd never been the kind of guy who loved women's company but Leanna, she was different. They had spent a couple of nights together watching movies, or going out with Strawberry. He couldn't believe his kid was going to school soon.

"Any news on Suz?" Knuckles asked, standing in the center of the large garden. Crazy saw himself, Strawberry, and Leanna living here. It was a good place to raise a kid, and to just have some fun.

A couple more kids.

He wanted more children with Leanna. The very thought of her stomach being swollen with his kid turned him on. Part of him didn't want her to get on the pill because he wanted her pregnant. Instead of arguing with her, he decided to respect her decision.

"She has called and wants me to make the drop,

and leave. Told her no, and she's been quiet since."

Crazy didn't like Suz quiet. She was plotting something, but he didn't have a fucking clue as to what.

"I hate bitches who try to take power."

"Suz was always a bitch." Crazy looked back at the house, and nodded. "This is the one."

"You sure?" Daisy asked. "This is our fourth house."

"I'm sure. It's the one." He walked to the realtor, placed an offer and gave instruction on what to do, and made his way out of the house.

Pulling out his cell phone, excitement filled him as he placed a call to his woman.

"Hello," Leanna said, sounding a little unsure.

"Hey, baby. I've got something to tell you. Where are you?"

"I'm at the park with Strawberry, why?"

"I'm coming to you. Don't go anywhere."

"Okay."

He slid into the car just as Daisy and Knuckles did.

"Do you want me to drop you off at the clubhouse?" he asked.

"You've got to be kidding me," Daisy said. "I want to see you make a fool of yourself."

"I'm with him."

Rolling his eyes, Crazy started up the car and headed toward the park. It wasn't that far from the main apartment building. He found Leanna standing behind Strawberry, who was on the swings. The moment Leanna spotted him, she stopped pushing Strawberry and helped her off the swings.

"What's up?" Leanna asked.

Cupping her face, he pressed a kiss to her lips before he said anything.

"Wow." She sighed, and smiled up at him.

"I found a place."

"A place?"

"Yes, a place for you, me, and Strawberry."

"You want us to move in together."

"Yes. Together, as a family."

Leanna smiled. "You're moving fast."

"I'm even prepared to hire a nanny so you know I'm not using you."

She chuckled. "No, I wouldn't trust anyone with Strawberry." She looked toward the little girl. "I kind of think of her as my own."

"Good. She's more yours than Suz's." He pressed his head to Leanna's. "You moving in?"

"Yes."

"Well, isn't this fucking nice!"

Crazy tensed as he recognized Suz's face. Turning his head, he saw his ex standing a foot away from them. Daisy and Knuckles had been distracted by a couple of women who were flirting with them. It was a fucking park, and none of them had expected any kind of danger.

"What are you doing here?" Crazy asked.

"You didn't give me my money, and now I'm telling you pay me, or my competition dies."

He froze as Suz pointed a gun at Leanna.

"Suz, what the hell are you doing? This is a park," Leanna said. The panic in her voice was clear to hear.

Someone in the background screamed, and Crazy saw they had a sudden audience. Knuckles and Daisy were ushering the few women who were at the park away from the danger. Suz had a gun, and was fucking dangerous. None of them could attack her and risk someone being hurt, or worse, killed. That bitch had the gun trained on Leanna.

"I don't give a fuck. I want my money. I really can't believe you've taken up with that fat bitch. You're mine, Crazy."

"I'm not yours, Suz. I never was. Put the gun down. You're not making it out of town, Suz. Think about this shit," Crazy said.

He didn't like how off the rails Suz had become.

When you were married, you controlled her.

Crazy had made a mistake. He should never have let Suz out of his sight. She would have been better controlled six feet fucking under.

"I see you two are screwing each other now. I knew it wasn't going to be long. I should have known you like fat bitches. You never could satisfy me."

He wanted to hurt the woman in front of him. When he got his hands on her, she was going to be dead.

Moving his hand behind his back, he went for the gun he always kept on him.

Suz tutted. "Keep your hands where I can see them. You think I don't know what you've got hiding behind you? Put them up. You better make sure those fuckers don't try to stop me. I can kill Leanna before they take me out."

"You can't do this, Suz," Leanna said.

"Shut up."

"Put the damn gun down. There are kids here," Crazy said, stepping closer.

"Don't even think of taking this off me. You fucking ruined me, you piece of shit. You and that club. You're nothing, you're fucking scum, and she's an ugly fat bitch who is taking what belongs to me. It's mine."

He saw her lose control, and before he could stop her, she fired three bullets. Crazy expected to feel the pain, but it was nothing. Suz gasped and stared past his shoulder. Leanna was no longer standing, and when he looked at the ground, his world fell apart.

Leanna held her hand to her chest, and she was gasping.

Daisy tackled Suz to the ground, and Crazy went to the woman he loved.

"It hurts," Leanna said, panting.

"Fuck, baby, someone call an ambulance." He didn't know what to do. She was bleeding, and he couldn't stop it.

"We can get her to the hospital," Knuckles said.

"What about Strawberry? What about Daisy?"

"Let us handle that. Get in your car, and take Leanna to the hospital now."

"Crazy?" Leanna said.

Lifting his woman into his arms, he ran toward his car, and shoved her into the car. Rushing to the driver's side, he climbed in, and pushed his foot to the gas, rushing out of the parking lot.

"Don't you die on me, Leanna. I need you."

He fucking loved her, and it wasn't just because of the past week, it was because of everything else. Crazy had been falling in love with her from the first moment he met her all those years ago when he'd first moved into the apartment building. He'd never acted on it because he'd been married, and Suz was spiteful enough to hurt Leanna.

She's shot her!

You could lose her.

Crazy screamed and pushed his foot on the accelerator.

Leanna gasped, and he glanced in the mirror to find the blood soaking her shirt. Tears streamed down his face, and he was hurting inside.

"Don't die on me, Leanna. I've got plans, baby.

Big plans. I love you, baby. I love you so damn much, and I'm going to make sure we have a family. You're not just a mother for Strawberry. I was so blind to the truth. Do you hear me? I love you. We're going to have a family, and you're never going to want for anything, I swear. You won't know what is going on with the love I'm going to give you. You're going to have the club by your side, and you're going to be protected."

He kept on talking, reaching behind him to grasp her hand. She was still with him, but her hand was slick with blood.

Pulling into the hospital emergency entrance, he almost went crashing into the door but brought the car to a stop without touching the glass. Climbing out, he yanked the door open, and tugged Leanna into his arms.

"Help! Someone help me!" He screamed for help, and nurses came running toward him.

"Tell me what's happening."

A bed magically appeared, and Crazy placed Leanna, who was no longer conscious, on the bed.

"She's been shot twice, maybe three times. I can't remember. My ex shot her in the park. Save her please."

"Sir, you need to step back."

"I've got to be with her."

"This woman is in critical condition. You have to step back and allow us to do our jobs."

A woman and several security men held him back.

"That's my woman there."

The woman tapped his chest. "We know, and we're going to do everything we can to save her. These moments count more than anything else. Sir, take a deep breath, go to the reception desk, and fill in the information we're going to need."

He stared at the woman, and nodded. "Okay."

"Okay. I will keep you updated, do you understand?"

"Yes, I understand."

"Good."

The nurse nodded at the guards, and Crazy took a step back. He needed to get his shit together. Leanna was shot, possibly dying, and she didn't need him going a little crazy in the one place that could save her.

Going to the receptionist, he got the necessary documentation, and took a seat. Holding the pen over the paperwork, he came up with a blank. He didn't know what to write, and time passed.

He didn't know how much time had passed, and suddenly someone touched his shoulder. Looking up he saw Duke, Pike, Daisy, Knuckles, Pie, and all of his brothers entering the hospital.

"What do you need?" Duke asked.

Crazy wiped away the tears that had been running down his face. "I don't know." Staring straight ahead, he took a deep breath. "I found the house. It was going to be perfect, and I was going to take Leanna and Strawberry to dinner. Strawberry?"

"Holly and Mary have her. They're taking care of all of the kids," Duke said. "You don't need to worry. We've got your back."

"My back. Yes. You've got my back. I was going to celebrate us moving in together. Leanna agreed to move in with me, and tonight I was going to make love to her. Strawberry knows we're together, and I've got a lock now, and I can take Leanna any way I want." He tapped the pen on the notepad, and kept on talking. "It was going to be perfect, and she shot her. I couldn't stop her. It should have been me that was shot. No one else."

Daisy took a seat beside him, and took the paperwork. "I'll fill this in."

"Who's keeping an eye on Suz?" Crazy asked. He was going to kill the bitch. He was going to wrap his fingers around her scrawny neck, and he was going to watch the life burn out of her. There was no way he was going to let her get away with what she'd done to him, and to his family.

"Russ and a couple of guys stayed behind. She's in the basement, and we've locked her up tight. She's not getting out."

Crazy nodded. "I deal with her."

Running fingers through his hair, he saw the dried blood on his hands, and without holding back, a whimper escaped him.

"You need to go and clean up," Duke said. "Knuckles, go with him."

Getting to his feet, he started walking toward the bathroom, but he stopped. "If you hear anything, you come and get me."

"I wouldn't do anything else."

Nodding, Crazy walked to the bathroom.

****

"There were a couple of witnesses at the park," Daisy said. "There's no way he can handle Suz without going down for that shit."

"The sheriff will be on your ass," Pie said.

"I'm not going to let anything happen to Crazy."

"He will kill her." Daisy recognized the crazy look in his friend's eye. It was the reason he'd gotten the name, Crazy. He was a mean motherfucker when he started, and Leanna being shot, it was a damn good reason for the guy to go off the rails.

"I'll deal with Crazy and Suz. I will not let a brother go to prison for that slut. What else do we know?"

"We don't. Leanna was shot by Suz, and there

was no time for an ambulance. Myself and Knuckles dealt with the situation." Daisy took a breath. He'd been flirting with one of the women at the park who was there with her kid. The one time his attention had been diverted, and his brother was suffering for it. It was just one fucking time. He never let his guard down, never. This was a reason why he never did.

Duke took a seat.

"What do we do now?" Raoul asked.

"We give our brother the support he needs. It's going to be a long couple of days."

Daisy stared at their president, Duke, and not for the first time was thankful he didn't have his job. Duke ran the Trojans with an iron first, but he also allowed them the space and freedom to do what they wanted without going to prison. All of the guys respected Duke for keeping the club safe, and out of trouble.

"Has Diaz had any news?" Duke asked.

Diaz was the club's contact, and connection to the group of Mexicans who wanted their drugs run through the States. Raoul was the one who dealt with Diaz, and often got them information they needed like this.

"About Suz?"

"She was high on something," Daisy said, recalling the way she was twitching, and her arms had been messed up.

"I talked to Diaz on the way over. No one would go near Suz. He said she was fucking tripping, but she was kicked out of their territory a few weeks ago," Raoul said.

"He got any other information for us?" Duke asked.

"Not as yet. We got another planned run in three weeks, and he wants to plan a meet to make sure everything is fine."

Duke tapped his knee. "Okay. Set up the meet in three weeks."

"Crazy's not going to be in any fit state to make a run," Pike said. "His girl don't make it, he's going to prison. None of us will be able to stop him from taking out Suz."

"Then we make sure he's locked down. My boy isn't going to prison for that slut." Duke stood, pacing. "Crazy's serious about the girl. I saw the way he was with her at the clubhouse. I've never known Crazy to be like that. He's in love with her."

Daisy couldn't argue.

"Right, we've got to take this one step at a time. Diaz owns the drugs, so Suz must have gotten them from a low time dealer. That's not a problem. It explains why she reached out for money. She needed to fund her habit. Seeing Leanna at the park, it was all set to scare her. We don't have any scores to settle."

Daisy agreed with Duke. There was no way this was a planned attack. It was sloppy, and it was more a vendetta than anything else, orchestrated by a crazy, jealous ex.

"We take it one step at a time," Daisy said.

They all agreed.

It was all they could do.

Chapter Ten

"Are you okay, man?" Knuckles asked.

"I've got blood from the woman I love more than anything on my hands. What do you think?" Crazy asked, entering the bathroom.

Knuckles followed behind him, and Crazy moved toward the sink, staring at his reflection. Even to himself, he saw the crazy assed look in his eyes. There were spots of blood on his face, and his shirt was covered. Tugging his shirt off, he threw it into the trash. Grabbing the bar of soap, he started to wash his hands.

Leanna's blood covered his hands and arms.

Swallowing past the lump in his throat, he watched the water turn red as it washed off his skin.

"You must think I'm a pussy."

"No, I don't."

"I'm crying. I'm fucking weak."

Staring at Knuckles in the mirror, he watched him shake his head. "I don't think you're weak. You picked your woman up who was shot and bleeding. This isn't just some random person, Crazy. Leanna's your woman. She belongs to you. You're not weak, and I don't think less of you. I envy you."

"You envy me? What the fuck have I got for you to envy? I'm divorced. I've got a kid with a slut I don't like. The same woman has just tried to kill, and may have been successful in killing, the woman I love. What the fuck do you have to envy? My life is fucking shit."

"You've got a woman that loves you back. Leanna may not have said it to you, but she does. I saw it at the barbeque, and at the park. She was happy with moving in with you. I don't have that. I've got club whores who want my cock, and nothing else. Believe me,

Crazy, you've got a lot for me to envy. I'm never going to have that."

He was speechless.

Knuckles didn't strike him as the kind of guy to be sentimental.

"I'm sorry."

"Don't be. I'm not the one hurting, but if I could change with you right now, I would. I'd do anything to spare a brother pain. I love my club. I love my brothers. I've got more than some men. I just don't have a woman of my own." Knuckles shrugged. "Not many women could handle me."

Crazy didn't need to ask what he was talking about. Knuckles had a reputation for being a sadistic bastard. He liked to tie women up, spank them, and use knives on them. Crazy didn't know if he made them bleed, and he didn't want to know. What got a brother off, had nothing to do with him.

"We're all a little fucked up," Crazy said.

"I hope Leanna makes it. I really do."

Walking back through the hospital, Crazy didn't give a fuck that he did so without a shirt. Sitting down with his brothers, he stared at the door that his woman had disappeared through. His brothers were silent, and the only sounds he heard were those of the updates coming over the intercom, along with nurses calling patients through.

Time passed.

He didn't know how much, and with each passing second, he was growing more and more frightened.

Finally, the door opened, and he didn't even know how long it had been when the nurse, followed by a doctor, walked through the door.

Getting to his feet, he stared at their grim expressions.

Don't be dead.
Don't be dead.
Don't be dead.
Don't be dead.

"Is she okay? Is Leanna okay?" He looked from the nurse to the doctor.

"Are you her next of kin?"

"I'm her fiancé, damn it. Is she okay? I brought her here. There wasn't enough time to wait."

Had he done the right thing?

"Leanna is stable at the moment," the doctor said. "She suffered three gunshot wounds. One missed her heart, and went straight through, thankfully not damaging any major artery. We repaired the damage. Another caught her side, and again, not life threatening. The last bullet pierced her lung causing her lung to collapse. We have repaired the damage, and it seems to be holding well. We will be monitoring her for the next couple of days. At the moment she's been given a sedative to help her rest."

"She's not in a coma?" Crazy asked.

"No. She lost consciousness from the blood loss, and pain. I don't want to give you any false hope, but her vitals are looking good."

"I want to see her. Please, I have to see her."

The doctor looked behind him.

"Only you can see her."

"Then I want to see her." Crazy couldn't go another minute without his woman.

"I'll take you through." The nurse spoke up, giving him a smile.

"We will monitor her closely." The doctor nodded at him before leaving.

Crazy followed the nurse, who pointed him to the room.

"She will look pale, and there will be a lot of tubes around her body, but they are there to help. Don't think she's in a bad condition. We've done everything we can to save her."

"I got here as fast as I could," Crazy said.

"I know. You were right. If you had waited for the ambulance, she would have died. Her lung collapsed on the way to the hospital, so those precious moments meant we could repair her lung. Ten minutes longer, and she wouldn't have survived the blood loss, and the lack of oxygen because of her collapsed lung would have caused severe brain damage."

"You're saying I did the right thing?" he asked.

"Some people think it's best to wait for the ambulance, and in a lot of cases, it's true. In others, lives are saved by people reacting rather than waiting. In this case, she was saved by you reacting. She's in there."

Crazy nodded, entering the room.

A sob escaped him as he looked at the woman he loved with all of his heart.

A tube was coming out of the side of her mouth, and her body was hooked up to three different machines.

"It's not that bad, I promise." The nurse walked over, and pointed at the screen. "This is monitoring her blood pressure, this one her pulse. We're monitoring her lung, and also keeping her hooked up to morphine to help with the pain."

"Why are you helping?" he asked, looking toward the nurse.

"I was there when you ran into the hospital. You looked so scared, and I don't know, you reminded me a little of my late brother."

"Late brother?"

"He died a couple of years ago during a robbery in a diner. It was a long time ago. I wanted to help. I know what it's like to lose a loved one, and no one seems to care. I care. It's why I became a nurse."

"What's your name?" Crazy asked.

"Kasey. Kasey Lintel."

"I'm Crazy."

"It's nice to meet you." Kasey gave him a smile, and turned back to the machines. "Her vitals are good, and the morphine will stop her from feeling any pain."

"Do you know when she'll wake up?"

"When the sedatives wear off she should come to. We'll monitor her pain level, and if need be, we will sedate her for another day. It's not our mission to cause pain, but to heal it."

"I'm in your debt," he said.

"You're not in my debt. Not in any way." She smiled, and moved to leave the room. "I'll be at the desk. Shout if you need me."

"Thank you."

Kasey didn't respond, and she left him alone.

"Hey, baby, you look fucking awful." He went to sit on the bed, and stopped himself. "Your pain is being controlled, so I'm not going to do anything to cause you more pain." Taking a seat on the bed, he took a breath. "I'm so sorry."

He touched her hand, and he was surprised to find her warm. She looked so pale and weak, he expected her to be cold.

"I don't know what to say to you. I want to say so much."

Silence fell on the room, apart from those machines beeping and making noises.

"I love you, Leanna. I love you so damn much, and I never got the chance to tell you." He chuckled. "Not that you would believe me. You'd think I was doing it to get into your pants. I didn't need to tell you I loved you to get into your pants. You're mine in every way."

Taking a deep breath, he leaned up, and pressed a kiss to her lips. She didn't respond, and he didn't think she would.

"We're going to get past this. There's no way I'm letting you get away from me now. You're going to marry me, and we're going to have a honeymoon that is so damn perfect. I'm going to spend every single day making love to you. In time Strawberry will need a brother or sister, or both. I'd be happy with a big family, and I bet you will, too."

Time passed, and Crazy kept talking to her, remembering moments he loved. He kept reaching up, and kissing her lips, holding her hand.

Kasey cleared her throat, and he turned to the door.

"I'm sorry to disturb you. Your friends wanted an update? I was also asked to say Strawberry. I don't know what that means."

"Strawberry's my daughter." He held Leanna's hand tightly. "I don't want to leave her."

"She will rest, and I will make sure the others know that you can come in at anytime if you'd like?" Kasey asked.

"I can come back?"

"Yes. You can come and sit with her."

"I want to be with her. I don't want to leave her alone." He kissed Leanna's hand. "Can I let one of the guys stay with her until I get back?"

Kasey nodded. "I will handle it."

"Okay. Okay. Baby, I'm going to let Daisy stay with you, and I'm going to go and talk to Strawberry, okay? She's going to be so worried about you. Stay here, rest, and get better. We've got a life to plan."

Kissing her hand, he moved up, and pressed

another kiss to her lips.

Opening and clenching his hands, he followed Kasey out to his brothers.

"I want someone to stay with Leanna," Crazy said, talking directly to Duke.

"Sure. Who do you want?"

He looked toward Daisy. "Will you stay with her?"

"Yes. I'll stay with her."

"I'm going to go back and talk to Strawberry. Kasey will show you where to go."

Daisy got up, shook his hand, and slapped him on the back. "I'll protect her."

He watched Daisy go, and wished it was him going to take care of his woman. He didn't like relying on anyone else but himself.

"I've got to go to Strawberry. She'll be worried."

"She's at the ranch with Mary and Holly," Pike said.

Exiting the hospital, he walked to his car that had been moved from the entrance of the hospital.

"I moved it for you," Knuckles said.

Crazy opened the back door of the car, and saw the bloodstains on the seat. His stomach turned, and in his mind he saw Leanna struggling for breath.

"I'm not going to the ranch." He moved to the front of his car. "I'm going to kill Suz."

Climbing into the car, he rode out of the parking lot, with the brothers quickly climbing onto their bikes to follow him.

For the second time that day, Crazy broke speed limits to get to the bitch who had tried to take his woman from him.

****

"Fuck! Follow him!" Duke rushed to his bike,

and straddled the machine. He followed the brother who was intent on ruining his life. Duke had killed his ex-wife when she took Holly, and almost got her killed. There was a huge difference between himself and Crazy. His woman hadn't made a public attack on Holly.

As far as anyone knew, his ex was off causing trouble elsewhere. There was no body that was going to be unearthed. Duke had taken care of it.

Crazy's woman had attacked Leanna in front of witnesses. People knew Suz, and the bitch had left a trail of evidence that would lead all the way back to Crazy. He couldn't have his man acting out now.

Pike moved beside him, and the rest of his men pulled up the rear. Crazy had a few minutes on them, and whatever speed limit he broke. Duke rode hard, but it wouldn't do for him to end up dead because he didn't drive safely. He was so fucking angry at himself. Duke should have taken the keys out of the ignition, but Knuckles had left them in. If they didn't get there in time, Crazy was going to ruin his entire life, and Duke wasn't going to let that happen.

Pulling into the parking lot, he saw Crazy was already scaring the shit out of everyone. The club whores were gathered together holding each other. Slowing his bike to a stop, Duke climbed off, letting the machine fall to the floor.

Crazy charged out of the clubhouse holding Suz around the neck. Duke saw her face was red from where he'd hit her.

"Crazy, man, you've got to stop," Duke said, getting closer.

There was no one listening in Crazy's mind. He dragged Suz over to the car. "You fucking see that! Her fucking blood, you fucking whore."

He watched as Crazy slammed her face into the

blood smeared upholstery, rubbing her face in it.

"She's a better woman than you'll ever be, and you nearly took her fucking away from me." Crazy tugged Suz out and slammed her against the car.

"I did you a favor. That fat bitch couldn't handle you." Suz laughed, and Duke couldn't believe she was doing this. Crazy had lost it, and was now the man who'd earned his name.

Crazy wrapped his fingers around Suz's throat and squeezed tightly. Suz started to claw at his arms, but Crazy wasn't letting go.

"You think you can handle me. You don't even know who you're dealing with."

The sound of the sheriff's car pulling up had Duke cursing. This wasn't something he needed to deal with.

"Go to the club safe. You know the combination. Get a hundred grand out. We're going to need it," Duke said, talking to Raoul.

The brother left, and Duke looked behind him to see Sheriff David going for his gun.

The women screamed as Crazy released Suz, but before the woman could catch her breath, he hauled her up by her hair, and dragged her toward the back of the clubhouse.

"Crazy, let her go," David, the sheriff, said, shouting.

Crazy didn't listen.

"What the fuck is going on?" David asked.

"Suz shot and almost killed Crazy's woman. Leanna, the babysitter at the apartment block?"

"I know who she is."

"She's in the hospital, and it's bad," Duke said.

"I can't look the other way, Duke. There are witnesses, and I've already taken their statements. The gunshot wound has been reported in the hospital. I can't just make it go away."

Duke cursed. "What if Crazy doesn't kill Suz? I get him to stop, no charges brought to Crazy?"

"Suz got roughed up by her drug dealers. I can write that down. Most of the witnesses stated that Suz looked high. Get him to stop, Duke. I can't do much more."

"Follow me." Duke moved toward Crazy, who was shouting once again.

Suz was on the floor kneeling, and it looked like she finally realized the dire situation that she was in. Tears were falling from her eyes, along with snot. She looked a mess. Crazy had a gun pointed to her head, and his finger was pressing against the trigger.

"Crazy, stop!"

Crazy hesitated, and glanced back at him.

"She's got to die, Duke. She's a problem, and I know how to deal with problems."

"There were witnesses, Crazy. She's going down, and she will go to prison."

"I don't believe in prison. Bitches like her will get parole. They all get parole." He pressed the barrel of the gun against her head. "She needs to die."

"You die, and who is going to look after Strawberry?"

"She'll go to Leanna."

"No, she won't. Leanna doesn't have a claim to her. She'll be put in the system, and we'll struggle to get her back. Leanna will be alone. You'll have lost everything. Put the gun away, and think, Crazy. Today, you can't win. No one can win today if you fire that gun. You put it away, and Suz goes away. You'll go and hold your little girl, and then visit Leanna. She needs you. How do you think she'll feel when she wakes up, and discovers you're gone?" Duke asked.

"Stop it."

"You know I'm right. Think about yourself, your loved ones, and the club. The Trojans will live to fight another day." He brought the Trojans up for Crazy to realize that Duke already had another plan.

Crazy looked behind him again. "What?"

"We're the Trojans MC. We live to fight another day, and to know when to put the guns down."

They were named Trojans for a reason. They had a way of getting the job done in other ways. The club had contacts, including Diaz, who knew how to get drugs and shit into prisons. Suz's days would be numbered, and it wouldn't fall back on the club.

"You promise?"

"My word."

Crazy released the gun and held it out for Duke. "Take her, Sheriff."

The next couple of minutes saw Suz screaming and begging for the sheriff to let her go, offering her body in exchange for freedom. Once Suz was in the backseat, cuffed, and restrained, Sheriff David walked back to them. Duke took the money from Raoul, and handed it to David. "Thank you."

David pocketed the money, and took the problem away with him.

"I want her dead."

"She'll be dead, but give it a couple of months of her in prison."

He'd do what needed to be done to keep Crazy's ass out of jail.

Chapter Eleven

Crazy washed and cleaned up at the clubhouse. His hands were shaking, but he started to calm down. It had taken a long time to get over the anger. When he saw Strawberry, he didn't want to have any remains of the anger.

Walking down to the main part of the club, he saw the brothers waiting for him.

"Thank you," he said, talking to Duke.

"You're welcome. We have to know when to walk away and when to stay and fight."

"Why did you stop me? You killed your ex?"

"I didn't have witnesses to silence. Suz did everything where there were adult and children witnesses. I don't kill or silence kids, Crazy. I'm a bad guy, but I'm not a monster. I'll never kill kids."

Crazy nodded. "I couldn't kill kids." Running a hand down his face, he chuckled. "I can't even begin to believe the kind of shit I'm going through right now. I'm going to see my kid."

He walked outside and straddled his bike, but he didn't start it up right away. Staring at the car, he nodded toward it. "Get the prospects to clean it, change the interior. I'll pay for all the work to be done."

Duke shouted the order, and Crazy didn't stay behind to hear what had to be said. He started making his way toward the ranch where Holly and Duke lived with their children. The open road didn't calm him down.

He was in turmoil, and he wanted his woman back in his arms. The sound of bikes pulling up behind him didn't cheer him up. Crazy shouldn't be driving to his daughter to tell her that Leanna was okay, and then to the hospital. They should be celebrating.

Fight another day.

Don't let Suz win.

If he shot Suz then he was fucked no matter what the club did. He couldn't make Suz disappear when there were enough witnesses to say that they had seen the Trojans holding her.

Riding down the long road to the ranch, he parked his bike, and ran up the steps. Holly was opening the door as he lifted his hand to knock.

"Is she okay?" Holly asked.

"She's stable at the moment but critical."

Holly wrapped her arms around him. "Anything we can do, let me know. We'll do whatever we can."

"Thank you. I appreciate it."

"Strawberry's in the kitchen with Mary and Matthew. We had to distract her. She was worried."

"I can imagine."

He walked past Holly and went straight to the kitchen. His daughter was standing on a stool, mixing something in a bowl. Mary had on a small television that was showing them how to make cupcakes. Leaning against the door, Crazy took a breath. The small sound alerted his daughter, and Strawberry dropped the bowl, and rushed toward him.

"Daddy!" She screamed his name and rushed to his side.

Bending down, he picked her up in his arms, and held her close to him. "I've got you, honey."

Mary picked up the bowl and started to clean up the mess Strawberry had made by dropping the bowl.

"I'm sorry," he said.

She held her hand up. "Don't even think of apologizing."

He nodded, and tears filled his eyes, which he forced down. He wasn't going to let this happen again.

Crying wasn't going to resolve anything.

"How is Leanna?"

"She's good, honey. She's going to need you to be a big girl though. Do you think you can do that for me?" he asked.

"I want to see her."

"Not today. She's very tired today. You're going to stay with Mary and Holly for a little while."

"But, Daddy!"

"No, honey. We've both got to be strong for her. We need to work together so Leanna can come home to us. Please, Strawberry."

"Mommy's mean."

"I know, but we don't need to worry about Mommy anymore. Don't think about her, okay? She's been naughty, and we can't help people who have been naughty."

"Okay, Daddy."

He held Strawberry close. Kissing her cheek, he picked her up, and looked at Mary. "Will you take care of her for me?"

"Of course. Holly and I will do it."

"We'll be glad to."

"I may need you to get some things from Leanna's apartment. I don't know when she'll be out of the hospital. I put an offer in on the house, and I've got that to deal with."

"We're all here for you. Duke will take over the purchase of your house. You've got the whole of the club on your side, Crazy," Holly said. "Tell us what you need."

"Thank you." He gave Strawberry a big squeeze. "Be a big girl for me, okay, and I will let you see Leanna the moment she's not tired anymore."

"Okay."

It was going to cost him a lot of presents.

A couple of minutes later he was leaving the ranch and riding toward the hospital. Parking his bike, he made his way to Leanna's room, and found Daisy was playing on his phone when he entered. The moment he was at the door, Daisy was ready to spring into action.

"How has she been?" Crazy asked.

"No change. That nurse who showed me to the room has been in twice to check on her vitals, and said it looks good."

"Thank you, Daisy."

"No problem. I like Leanna." Daisy got to his feet. "Do you need me to stay?"

"No. I've got it from here. You can go back to the clubhouse."

"We're here if you need us."

"Thank you." Crazy took the seat that Daisy had been sitting in. He was tired, and in need of some rest.

Rubbing his eyes, he moved the chair to Leanna's side, taking hold of her hand. He grabbed the remote, and aimed it up at the television. Listening to those damn machines was going to send him to an early grave, and he wasn't interested in going to an early grave.

He had a lot of plans.

Watching the television, he sat through a crime drama, and then a supernatural one about vampires. Kasey brought him some food after she checked Leanna's vitals.

"I'm clocking off shift in ten minutes. I've left notes for the nurse who'll take over." She gave him a smile. "Leanna's holding in there, I promise. She's strong."

"I know she is."

"I'll see you tomorrow."

He ate the food, and rested his head on the bed,

watching the television. The hours passed, and it wasn't long before sleep claimed him.

Crazy didn't know how long he'd been asleep before he was woken up by Leanna's hand moving.

Jerking up, he looked at his woman, and stared into her beautiful brown eyes. Leanna was staring at him, and Crazy's heart raced.

"Hey, baby."

She wasn't waking up so well, and her hand went to the pipe in her mouth. Slamming his hand on the alarm, he shouted for good measure.

"Leanna, baby, calm down. You can't tear it out."

He tried to get her hands, but she was fighting it.

Two nurses rushed in, and he watched them taking over, removing the pipe from her mouth.

Leanna took a deep breath, choking.

"Leanna, you need to calm down. You've had surgery, and we need you to relax so you don't break your stitches."

The nurses started talking, and Leanna's eyes were panicked.

"Crazy?" She called his name, and it was in a croak.

Moving the nurse out of the way, he took Leanna's hand, kissing her.

"I'm here, baby. I'm here, and I'm not going away."

The nurses started checking her vitals and noting down their findings.

"We need to get the doctor."

"Water," Leanna said.

Grabbing the pitcher, he poured some water into the glass, and pressed the straw to her lips. She took a sip, and winced.

"I hurt."

"You're alive."

"I remember what happened," she said. Her voice sounded raw as if she'd been screaming. Leanna tightened her hand around his. "You saved me."

"I got you here. The nurses and doctors saved you."

"Thank you. I didn't want to die. I don't want to die."

He held her hand a little tighter. "I'm not going to let you die, baby. We're here, and we're together."

She nodded, wincing again. "It hurts."

"Rest."

Leaning up, he kissed her lips, holding her hand. "I'm not going anywhere, and you need to be strong for Strawberry."

"How is she?"

"I will tell you everything when you're ready. Strawberry's fine. Everything is fine. We all need you to get stronger."

Leanna nodded. "Stronger. I can do stronger."

He chuckled, and for the first time in twenty-four hours, he really believed everything was going to be okay.

****

"Are you okay?" Maria asked.

Daisy turned toward his bed, surprised to see Maria sitting there. He'd not seen her when he entered the clubhouse.

"What are you doing here?"

"I heard what was going on. I was worried."

"Where's Beth?" He'd not been to see his sister, and he was worried about her. Suz shooting Leanna had put the club on edge. Duke had updated him on what happened. He was surprised that Crazy was able to hold back. He was a better man than all of them. None of them would have ever been able to hold back, and yet Crazy had.

"She's in her room. Beth knows what happened but said that we were to stay out of the way."

He had a towel wrapped around his waist, and the very sight of Maria had set his cock from flaccid to hard.

"Why are you here?" he asked.

Maria's cheeks were red, and she stared down at her lap. "I know you're not a monster. You pretend you are, but we know you're not."

Daisy laughed. "You think I'm not a monster? I'm part of the Trojans MC."

"And yet today you sat at a woman's side who means nothing to you."

"You're wrong."

"Leanna means something to you."

"She's an old lady. She'll mean something to the club when Crazy finally claims her." He wanted to sink his fingers into her silky dark hair, and slam his cock into her mouth. Daisy wanted Maria, but he'd done his best to stay away from her. She was a mixture of sweet and fiery.

"Why do you hide who you are?" Maria asked.

"Why are you determined to see a man that isn't there?"

"I don't believe you're as heartless as you make out."

"Then you're an idiot." Daisy knelt down, and stared into her eyes. "You don't have a clue who I am. You don't even know what I'm thinking right now."

"Daisy?"

"I'll tell you what I'm thinking. I want to grip your hair, hold you in place, and shove my dick into your mouth. I want tear the clothes you're wearing, and fuck you so damn hard that you're screaming for me to stop, and yet begging for more. I don't play games, Maria. I want to fuck you, and possess every inch of your body. The thing is, I'm not going to give you back. I stake my claim, and you're not going home. That's the kind of man I am. I will kill people for this club, and I will not hesitate. Once I take you, no other man will be allowed to look at you. I will own you."

Tears filled Maria's eyes.

"Get the fuck out of my room. You're not ready to handle the kind of man I am."

Maria rushed out of the room, and Daisy sat down on the edge of the bed. He wasn't ready to settle down, but the moment he'd stared into her startling green eyes, he wanted to lock her in his room and make her his.

He'd do whatever was necessary in order to take her, and to fuck her.

She's too innocent.

And for that reason, he was going to have to let her go. He wasn't good enough for Maria.
****

Maria closed her door and took a deep breath. Her heart was pounding, and her pussy was on fire. She wasn't afraid. She was aroused and needy.

Daisy had always been an enigma to her. He was her best friend's older brother, and Maria had been fantasizing about him for years. No other guy measured up to him, not in any way. It had been a couple of months since the last time she'd seen him, and she really thought that he didn't want her.

She was all over the place with her feelings for Daisy. One moment she hated him, the next moment she wanted him, and all the times in between. She'd tried dating other guys, and none of them even held a candle to Daisy.

The thought of being owned and claimed by

Daisy didn't scare or upset her. It was what she wanted, and she had tried to fight those feelings at all times. In the world where women were supposed to be fighting for her independence, Maria yearned for a man who would take care of her. Maria had witnessed her own parents in a similar relationship.

Ever since she'd become aware of sex, love, and she'd done research online, she'd paid attention. Her mother stayed at home, taking care of Maria, and providing a good home for her father, while her father earned the money, was the man who dealt with everything.

It had confused her at first.

Her parents were in a type of Dom/sub relationship.

She hadn't been repulsed by the idea. Of course, she'd been a little put out about her parents because that was just gross.

Doing more research, Maria had discovered a yearning within herself for the exact same thing, but she would need a man she could trust. Putting her life in the hands of someone else scared her.

Daisy had been the only guy who'd come close to being what Maria wanted.

Tears filled her eyes and fell down her cheeks. There was no way she was ever going to get what she wanted when she couldn't even handle Daisy being blunt with her. Maria was still a virgin, and she didn't want any other man to touch her.

"It's hopeless."

There was no chance of her ever finding what she wanted if she kept running from the man she really wanted.

Chapter Twelve

One week later

Leanna was in pain, but it was manageable. She was no longer hooked up to multiple machines, and she could finally go to the bathroom when she wanted, and not in a bag any longer. Crazy had gone to get Strawberry, and Daisy was sat with her.

"Are you okay?" she asked.

The biker was brooding, and she didn't know how to handle brooding bikers.

"I'm fine. Just got shit on my mind."

Sitting against the pillows she took a breath. The pain was still a little too much for her at times. She couldn't believe she had almost died, but then, she couldn't believe she had been shot.

"Do you want to share with me? I'm not going anywhere so you can share whatever you want, and I won't tell a soul."

She was bored. Lying in bed all day was boring. The television sucked, and she didn't have a clue what to do with her time.

"It's nothing, and I'm not going to talk about it."

"Okay."

"You know Crazy's going to marry you," Daisy said.

"He's said so."

Leanna smiled. It had been a strange week. Crazy rarely left her side, and even when the nurses came in to check her over, he was there, watching over her, and taking care of her in his own way. She loved it. He was so sweet.

"There's a woman that I want," Daisy said.

"You don't need to tell me if you don't want to."

"It's hard. I want something that I can't have."

"How do you know you can't have it?" Leanna asked.

"She would run if she knew what I wanted to do to her. She did run." He ran fingers through his hair. "Forget it."

"Take it easy. I wanted to run from Crazy. He made me want things that I had tried to bury. If you want something badly enough, be willing to compromise."

"I can't compromise. I don't want to."

Leanna tilted her head, watching him. "Then seduce her if you can. I don't know who you're talking about, but you seem like a nice enough man."

Daisy cursed.

"Hey," Holly said, walking into the room carrying several balloons.

Leanna chuckled, and winced. Her wounds were still giving her some trouble.

"What's all this?"

"Crazy's got Strawberry outside, but he said we were free to come inside, and bring gifts." Behind Holly were Mary and Zoe.

"We all got gifts," Zoe said.

"You didn't have to."

"Don't you know when you're ill, you're supposed to have gifts?" Holly said, tying the balloons around the bed.

"I don't think the nurses will be happy with them."

"Tough. I'm not taking them back."

Mary came to her side, carrying a boxed cake. "We made it, so don't worry about it being shop bought. This is much better."

"Thank you."

"And flowers. We didn't know what you liked. Also, we got you a bunch of books," Zoe said, placing them on the bed.

Opening the brown bag, Leanna looked in to find erotic titles. "I thought they invented e-readers for these?"

"You're ill and injured. This is much better."

Shaking her head, Leanna placed them on the drawer top beside her bed. "Thank you."

"We really hope you get better, and when you're out of the hospital, and ready, we're going to have a girly day. Think booze, food, and possibly a stripper," Holly said.

"Oh, I could get Landon to strip. He owes me after I came home to find his condom on my couch. I had to throw the couch out. What kind of man screws a woman on the couch?"

Leanna recalled her and Crazy's first date together. They'd ended up on the couch, and Crazy didn't get his happy moment.

Holly, Mary, and Zoe left. When Crazy and Strawberry entered the room, Daisy left.

Strawberry rushed to the bed, but before she could jump on the sheets, Crazy caught her. "She's still poorly, honey. Be careful."

She gave Crazy a smile.

"Sorry, Leanna."

"It's okay. How are you?"

She talked with the little girl, trying to hide her tiredness. The doctor had told her it would take her some time to get her strength back.

After half an hour, she gave in to her yawn, and Crazy made her say goodbye to Strawberry. She waved at the little girl, and instead of being alone, Crazy came back.

"Where's Strawberry?"

"She's spending the night with Russ and Sheila."

"You should go home. Go back to the apartment, and take care of her, Crazy. I'm not going anywhere."

"No. You were shot because of me. I'm here. I love you, Leanna."

She'd never get tired of hearing him say that. "I love you, too."

He took her hand and kissed her knuckles.

"I'm not going to be in the hospital forever."

"When you're out, we're getting married."

"How is the house going?"

"I should be able to move in soon, about three weeks."

"That's good."

"I've already started boxing up your apartment."

"What?"

"You heard me. We're moving in together, and you already agreed. We're getting married, and you're my old lady."

"I'm not that old."

"I know. It's a term of endearment. You don't have to worry about it at all." Crazy released a sigh. "There's something I've got to tell you."

"That sounds scary. You don't look happy about it."

"There's a way that I have to claim you in front of the club to make you my old lady. It's what Holly, Mary, and Zoe have been through, and other old ladies in the past."

"I'm not going to like this, am I?"

"I don't know, baby. You're adventurous, so it may answer one of those fantasies of yours."

"What is it?" she asked. She had a lot of fantasies, and many of them revolved around Crazy. In fact, all of her fantasies were all about Crazy, and featured Crazy in some way.

"Old ladies are taken in front of several members of the club. No one is allowed to touch her but the guy who is marking her as his."

"You mean sex?"

"Yes."

"In order for me to be considered yours by the club, you have to have sex with me?"

"Yes."

Leanna wasn't angry at him, and figured there had to be a reason that being an old lady was in fact special to the club. When Holly and Mary had talked about being an old lady, a look had come into their eyes, and she'd known it had been special to them.

"I'm not in the best condition for that, Crazy."

"I'm not joking about this."

"I know. Can we talk about this another time? I've been shot three times, and I'm in the hospital. I don't want to think about having sex while other men watch. Would you even want them to see you with me?" she asked, confused.

"What do you mean?"

"I'm not exactly hot stuff, or model material."

"Sweetheart, if you're putting yourself down, I can promise you, I will spank that ass."

"I'm injured."

"And I've got a damned good memory, precious. I'll remember them, and when you're better, I'll make sure you never put yourself down again."

Leanna huffed.

"I love you, and I think you've got a smoking hot body. There's no one else I want more than you. The guys will not touch you, and they will know that you belong to me."

Leanna didn't like the thought of being observed or watched by others. Seeing the need staring back at her, she would do it for Crazy.

****

Three weeks later

Crazy drove his newly upholstered car toward the hospital. Strawberry was in the back seat, excited at the fact they were finally taking Leanna home. The doctor had kept Leanna in as the patch on her lung had slipped, and he'd gone back into repair it. Nothing in the past three weeks had gone wrong, and Leanna was now fit and well.

Her injuries were patched up, and in a couple of weeks, the stitches would be removed. The doctor was happy for her to be discharged, providing she didn't do anything too strenuous. Crazy had gotten the doctor alone to make sure sex was still an option. Sex wouldn't be a problem. He just needed to consider Leanna when they had sex, which he would have done anyway. He didn't like that fucking doctor.

There was a huge surprise waiting for her when they got home, and he saw Strawberry in the back bursting with excitement.

"You don't say anything, okay? You can't tell Leanna."

"I know, Daddy. She's going to love it."

He chuckled.

Crazy really hoped she did. He was taking a big risk. In the last month since she'd been in the hospital, he felt that they had grown closer together as a couple. Leanna had opened up to him about her fears, and he'd opened up to her about what he wanted. Once he'd explained the way the club claimed a woman, he'd expected her to be so damn angry. She'd accepted it, but he saw she didn't like it.

The claiming of an old lady was the way the Trojans MC wanted it to be. Not only did it show the brothers within the club that a woman was off limits, it also showed what the woman was prepared to do for her man. It was a marriage of minds, bodies, souls, and strengths. The club brothers respected that.

Not all women had the confidence to be taken, fucked, made love to in front of a bunch of other men. By breaking down their fears, and doing it, being claimed as a member's property, they're gaining the respect of the club.

Yes, to some it didn't make sense.

To the club, it made all the sense it needed to. The club didn't need to justify its actions to anyone else, and it never would. He didn't know what the other clubs, like The Skulls, Chaos Bleeds, Dirty Fuckers MC, or the Saints and Sinners MC, did to accept new old ladies, club pussy, and prospects.

Crazy had only ever been interested in Trojans MC.

Pulling up outside of the hospital, Crazy was nervous as hell.

What if she said no?

What if today's planning had all been for nothing?

Don't think.

Just do.

He helped Strawberry out of the backseat, and together they made their way into the hospital. She gripped his hand a little tighter. His little girl had been so scared of Leanna not coming out of the hospital. He didn't know how to reassure her, so he'd not said much of anything.

Nodding his head toward Kasey, the nurse gave him a wave before turning her attention back to her client.

When he entered Leanna's room, he saw she was already packed and ready to go.

Strawberry rushed to her, throwing her hands around her legs.

"I missed you," Leanna said.

"Missed you."

Crazy stepped close, gripping the back of her neck, and pressing a harder kiss to her lips. "I missed you."

She gave him a smile.

"Can we get out of here? I've spent more time in the hospital than I ever wanted to."

"Sure. You're feeling good. Everything okay?"

"Yes. More than fine."

Crazy took her bags while Strawberry carried her bag with gifts. The club had been by several times giving her gifts, and offering her advice. He'd heard some of the club women sitting with her, and talking.

He was happy the club had accepted her so easily.

It helped that she was a wonderful woman with a great heart.

Leaving the hospital was a welcome relief. He'd not even been the one inside, but the moment he left the hospital doors, and took a breath of fresh air, he was in heaven. It was time to take his woman home.

Strawberry kept talking, and filling up any kind of silences. Placing all of her bags in the back, along with her gifts, he helped Leanna inside, doing her seatbelt up once again.

"I can do that."

"I want to do it for you."

He was behind the wheel, and driving toward their brand new home. Strawberry, his little girl, kept on talking, and Leanna in some way kept up with her. Crazy tuned out, hoping that the guys had the last minute preparations ready. He would have stayed behind, but he didn't want to risk this surprise being spoilt.

The drive didn't take too long, and Strawberry proved to be the perfect distraction. Parking outside of the house, Leanna gasped. "This is our place?"

"Yes, and I've got my own room, and so have you and Daddy," Strawberry said.

Leanna laughed. "It looks amazing. I can't wait to see what is inside."

With her bags in hand, they made their way toward the door. There was no sign of anyone, and Crazy's heart was pounding inside his chest. Placing her bags close to the stairs, Strawberry rushed toward the back of the house.

"What's wrong with her?"

"You know. She's excited about being a new house, new place, and lots of new problems."

"Are you okay, Crazy? Are you sure you're ready to move in together?"

"Yes. I'm more than ready. It's something else."

Leanna smiled. "What? I take a bullet for you, and you've got something else you want me to do."

He decided to just do it, and see what happened. Taking her hand, he led her toward the back of the house, toward the kitchen.

"I don't get a tour."

"You do, in a minute." He took a deep breath, and couldn't believe how nervous he was. More than anything he wanted her to say yes, so he could make her his woman completely.

Opening the door to the garden, he pulled her outside, and the whole Trojans gang shouted, "Surprise!"

Leanna gasped, and he saw her take in the garden. He'd left Holly and Sheila in charge to make it look perfect for a wedding day. There were white streamers hanging from the few trees. Chairs sat on either side, creating an aisle down the center.

Going to his knee, Crazy pulled the ring that had been burning within his pocket.

"Will you do me the honor of becoming my wife?"

"You did all of this for me?"

"Yes. I did it for us. I didn't think you'd want a church filled with strangers from town. The club is our family."

Tears fell from her eyes, and he hoped they were tears of happiness.

"You want to marry me?"

"Yes."

Leanna glanced down at herself. She was dressed in a blue summer dress, plain black pumps, with her hair tied behind her head.

"I look a mess."

"You look beautiful to me. Look at them, Leanna. They don't expect a perfect wedding. This is between us, and what we think is perfect."

"Yes," she said.

"You'll marry me."

"Yes. Today, right now, I'll marry you. I don't want to waste anther second."

Getting to his feet, he wrapped his arms around her, and took possession of her lips. "I'm going to make you the happiest woman in the world," he said.

"I look forward to you keeping that promise."

"It's not going to be hard." Rubbing his nose against hers, he ignored all the catcalls, and whistles from the club. "I can only get them to behave for so long."

"It's okay. I like it."

They made their way down the aisle, and he quickly handed Strawberry the keys. He'd gotten the priest to come and marry them away, while providing a huge donation to the local church.

The ceremony was straightforward, and neither of them had spent any time with their vows. What they spoke came from the heart.

"Leanna, I intend to love you, cherish you, and be with you through all the failures and successes. I will not leave you alone again. You're my life, my love, forever. There is no end for us."

"Crazy, I love you with my whole heart, and I love your daughter. I will try to be the perfect wife that you need, and be with you in everything that your heart desires."

He smiled, and touched her cheek. In no time at all, they were pronounced husband and wife, and he could finally kiss his bride.

The priest left his home after the ceremony, and Crazy thanked him for taking the time to stop by.

Leanna was embraced by the women, and he saw that Beth and Maria had come to the service.

Moving to the men, Duke slapped him on the back, Pike embraced him, Russ kissed him on both cheeks.

"Twice down the aisle, you think this is the one?" Daisy asked.

"Leanna was the only one. The other, she was the mistake." He looked over his shoulder to see Leanna smiling back at him. Tonight he was going to make to love her as his wife.

"Stop the dirty thoughts," Knuckles said. "Children are present."

"You're still good to watch Strawberry tonight?" he asked, directing his question at Duke.

"Of course."

"Good." It had been a month without touching his woman, and he intended to make sure tonight was special.

He took a bottle of beer that was passed to him. The music was turned on, and he took claim of his wife, tugging her away from the group of women, cooing over her.

Wrapping his arms around her, he rested his hand against her ass.

"I can't believe you did all of this for me."

"I wouldn't do it for anyone else. I love you."

"I love you, too. There's a sweet side to you that you keep hidden."

"Sh, I don't want the guys to know. I'd never live it down, and they would make my life a misery."

She threw her head back laughing. "I know, and I'm going to keep it to myself, and Strawberry."

"You do that."

Chapter Thirteen

Leanna looked around the kitchen, taking a sip of her orange juice. It was a beautiful house, and Holly had offered to come back tomorrow to clean up the mess. She couldn't believe this was her house. The house was so big, spacious, and as she moved from room to room, she fell in love with it.

Walking into the sitting room, she closed the curtains, and gasped as Crazy's arms went around her waist.

"What are you doing?" she asked, chuckling.

"The last of the guests have gone. I want you, Leanna. It has been too long." He kissed her neck, at the same time, his hand slid up the inside of her thigh. "Tonight is our night."

"I want you, too."

She moaned as his hand landed over her pussy. He slid his fingers beneath the fabric of her panties. Closing her eyes, she released a moan as he touched her clit, circling the bud before moving down to press inside her.

"You're wet, baby."

"Yes."

"This is how it's always going to be between us. You're going to be soaking wet, and I'm going to love every second of it."

In answer, she moaned. There was no other response as he plunged two fingers inside her.

He removed his fingers, and she turned to watch him sucking the cream from his digits.

"You taste perfect. Remove your clothes."

"You're always telling me to remove my clothes."

"Get used to it. I like getting my own way."

She took her dress off, and at the same time, Crazy got naked. The moment they were naked, he took her hand, and led the way toward the stairs. She hadn't been upstairs yet, and she couldn't wait to see their room.

Crazy picked her up when they were outside of their room, and she squealed as he picked her up, carrying her over the threshold.

"Our room awaits, baby."

He placed her down on the large bed, and Leanna loved what she saw of the room. Crazy didn't give her the chance to take anything in. His lips were on hers, but not for long. He kissed down her neck, to the top of her breasts. She moaned, wriggling underneath him, and begging for his touch.

"Please, I need you, Crazy."

There was no rushing him, and he kissed over each one of her bandages, which she found incredibly sweet. She sank her fingers into his hair.

He caught her hands, pressing them down beside her, holding her down. Watching his kiss down her stomach, he moved toward her side, placing a kiss to the final bandage. Crazy didn't stop him there, and moved to her stomach, going to her pussy.

"Open your legs."

She spread her thighs, and cried out as he took her clit, and sucked it deep into his mouth, using his teeth to create a small bite of pain. It was everything she wanted, and more. He moved down, fucking his tongue inside her.

Biting her lips, she thrust up to meet him, and he kept hold of her, keeping her exactly where he wanted her. His grip tightened around her wrists, turning her on.

"Please."

"Tell me to lick your pussy."

"Lick my pussy, Crazy."

Fucking his tongue back inside her, he moved up, gliding over her clit, then back down again. Over and over, he created more and more pleasure, heightening her arousal to the point of orgasm.

He released her and took a step back.

"Why? I was so close," she said, pouting.

Crazy wrapped his fingers around his dick, and slid his hand up and down the length. "Come and taste me."

She didn't need to be asked twice. Sinking to her knees, she crawled toward him, seeing the move had aroused him even more. Smiling, she wrapped her fingers around his length, and Crazy released his own dick. Taking over, she worked her fingers up and down his dick, tasting his pre-cum as she licked the tip. She didn't make him wait long before she took the whole length of him to the back of her throat.

He cursed, and his fingers were once again back in her hair. She swallowed him down, bobbing her head, and loving how she was able to give him the kind of pleasure that he loved.

"Fuck, baby, your mouth is so damn good. I've missed you. This last month has been a nightmare. I need you, and I want you." He thrust into her mouth, and Leanna opened her lips so that he could go as deep as he wanted. "Fuck, fuck, fuck."

Crazy tugged on her hair, and she pulled back, thrusting her chest up.

"I've got to have you."

She moved onto the bed, and Crazy made her pause. "Open your thighs."

Frowning, she opened her legs.

"Today, I want to come in your pussy, and watch as it fills it up."

"Crazy?"

"I love you, Leanna. I love you so damn much, and I'm not going to change who I am. I'm going to piss you off, probably upset you, but I will always come back to you."

Biting her lip, she opened her thighs. "Are you really ready to take the risk of having sex?"

"I want more kids with you. You're my life, and I know what I want. Trust me."

She did trust him. "Okay."

Leanna had been on the pill, but she didn't know how effective it was going to be with the pain medication that she had taken.

He ran his fingers against the inside of her thigh, and he touched her pussy, sliding two fingers inside her. "You're wetter, Leanna."

"I want you. It has been too long."

Crazy tugged her to the edge of the bed, and she watched him grab his cock, pressing the tip to her core. She gasped out as he pressed inside her, spreading her pussy wide. It had been too long since he'd been inside her, and she didn't know how she'd survived the last month.

"Look at us, Leanna, look as I take you."

She stared down at his cock as it slowly filled her pussy. Crying out, she couldn't look away as his length disappeared. He stretched her around his length, and she opened her thighs to accommodate him better.

Tonight was going to be the night of her life, her true wedding night.

****

Crazy was so close to coming already that he didn't know how he kept control. Leanna was so wet, and he felt every inch of her perfect pussy as he slid inside her. The walls of her cunt gripped him tightly.

Staring down at her tight pussy, he groaned. She was so perfect, and beautiful, and now she belonged to him. He was never giving her up.

"Please, Crazy."

"You want me to fuck you?" he asked.

"Yes." She screamed the one word at him, and he chuckled. Pulling out of her sweetness, he saw her cream had slicked his cock. When only the tip remained inside her, he slammed right up, and she groaned. He tugged her up so that her hands were wrapped around him. Her nails sinking into his shoulders, and he growled against the flesh of her neck, flicking his tongue against her pulse.

"I love you, Leanna. You belong to me."

It had been too long since he was inside her, and he didn't know how much longer he could hold off. Reaching between them, he fingered her clit, and fucked her at the same time.

She moaned, and with a few strokes of his fingers, she came around his length.

"I'm not going to last, baby. Fuck. This is fucking perfect. I need you. I'm going to fuck you again. I can't wait."

"Come inside me, Crazy," she said, whispering the words against his ear. "Fill me up with your cum."

Those words set him off, and he came, filling her up, and doing exactly what she said. When it was over, he rested his head against hers, and stayed inside her.

"That was short but amazing," she said, breathlessly.

"The night's not over. I'm going to be taking you again, and again. This is just the first one of many."

"What do you want me to do now?" Leanne leaned back staring into his eyes. "I want you to have everything you want. I don't want to ever worry about you running off to create your fantasies with another woman."

Crazy pressed a kiss to her lips, wanting more than anything to see her pussy leaking his cum, but he wanted to understand Leanna's change, so he asked.

"I almost died, Crazy. I could have died, and I'd not done half the stuff we were going to do. This is one of those things you want, and I want to know what it's like for you to claim every *hole*."

He burst out laughing at her delicate way of saying she wanted him to fuck her in the ass. Crazy was more than happy to oblige.

"When I woke up, I realized that I didn't want to die regretting all the things I hadn't done, especially when I can experience them now, with you. I love you, Crazy. I think I have from the first moment I saw you. I was scared. No other man has left me feeling the way you have."

"I'm the lucky son of a bitch who got to have you."

Releasing her arms, he lowered her back to the bed pressing a kiss to both of her tits. He pulled out of her pussy, and he watched as his white cream leaked out of her. Coating his fingers in his cum, he pressed them back inside her.

"I want you pregnant with my kid. I need to make it so that you can't walk away from me."

"I'm not going to walk away."

"Good. I'm going to fuck you until you're pregnant."

She chuckled. "You're not listening."

"I'm listening, but I'm going to do what I want."

He moved to the bathroom, grabbing a cloth, and returning to wipe away the excess. Crazy took care of her, and when he was finished, he took her hand.

"Time for that tour before I bring you back, and fuck you all over again." He tugged her to his side, resting his hand on her full, rounded hip.

"Did you and the guys decorate?"

"Yes. I wanted everything perfect." They left their room, and he led her toward the main family bathroom.

"It's big."

"You're going to be saying that a lot tonight."

Laughing, she rested her head on his.

"Strawberry called this room." He opened the door to reveal a pink, princess-covered bedroom.

Crazy had been the one to decorate it, and Strawberry had picked all the furniture she wanted.

"This is her dream bedroom. She talked about it all the time. What did happen to my apartment?" Leanna asked.

"Holly, Mary, Zoe, and Sheila helped us move all of your furniture out, and I paid the landlord the last of the rent. You're a wealthy woman, and you pay rent?"

"I didn't want to buy the apartment. I liked living there."

"I'm never going to understand you, am I?"

"I don't know. Do you want to?"

"Yes, I want to understand you. You're my woman, and I want to know what you're thinking and feeling."

He heard her sigh. "I guess, I was renting month by month in case I wanted a reason to leave quickly. I didn't want to deal with selling the apartment, and renting the space meant I could go whenever I wanted to."

"You became attached to Strawberry?"

"Yes. She's a sweet girl, and I cherished her. Suz, erm, Suz didn't seem to realize what an amazing daughter she had, and when she came to me, I wanted Strawberry to know what it was like to be loved."

"She does know. Believe me, she does."

Leanna nodded, resting her head against his shoulder. "Does she have a problem with me living with you two full time?"

"Are you kidding? Strawberry can't wait."

He took her hand, and kissed her fingers. "Don't be mad at me." Taking her to the next room, he opened the door, and flicked on the light.

She gasped, and he entered. "I went for neutral colors. I hope you don't mind."

It was a nursery, and he'd taken a lot of time to make sure it was perfectly done for either a boy or girl.

"You did this?"

"Yes. I wouldn't let anyone else into the room."

"I love it."

"I was hoping you'd like to start filling it as soon as possible."

"Yes, I will. I want to." She went into his arms, wrapping her arms around his neck, and kissing his lips. "Let's make a start tonight."

Gripping her ass, he chuckled. "We already have."

Chapter Fourteen

Three weeks later

Leanna was nervous as she paced the kitchen of the clubhouse. It was one of the final barbeques of the summer. It was the last weekend for Beth and Maria before they went back home, and next week Strawberry started school. Leanna had gotten the all clear from the hospital yesterday, but it wasn't that which had her nervous.

It was a clubhouse party for the Trojans MC, and Crazy had told her tonight he was going to make her an old lady. She stood in the kitchen with Holly, Mary, and Zoe. The other women were spread out either in the clubhouse or outside enjoying the barbeque. Leanna was pacing in front of the oven where she was waiting for her lasagna to finish baking.

Maria and Beth left the kitchen to take out some of the drinks that had been left on the table.

"How are you handing the wait?" Mary asked, coming to stand beside her. Holly was icing the cupcakes that had been made, and Zoe was eating the frosting. It was a battle between Holly and Zoe to see who could get the frosting finished first. There were a lot of cupcakes, and Holly was glaring at Zoe, who shrugged. "You shouldn't make good frosting. If it tasted bad, then I wouldn't be eating it."

"It's supposed to go on the cupcakes. The men will come after your ass, spanking it if I don't have enough to frost."

"Raoul will protect me."

"Ignore them. It always happens when Zoe's in the kitchen. She can't cook, so she eats everything we cook."

Leanna nodded. "I noticed."

"You're nervous."

"Weren't you?"

"Pike tried to claim me in front of the club without me knowing it."

She frowned. "How is that possible?"

"By making me so aroused that I wouldn't realize that I was about to be fucked in a club full of men. I ran out on him, and wouldn't talk to him for so long. He apologized, and it took me time to realize that it was a club thing for the men."

"Crazy explained it to me."

"It's not dirty," Zoe said. "The men don't look at you as if you're a tramp. None of them stare at you as if they've seen you naked either. It's a man club thing. I don't know why they do it."

"It's respect," Holly said. "We can't use our fists to gain the men's trust. We're all nervous about showing our bodies, and opening ourselves up during sex. Being an old lady in front of the club proves to the men you're willing to do what your man wants, you're protecting him. I know I'd protect Duke. I'd lie for him as well to protect him."

Leanna nodded. "Crazy talked to me about it last night. He wants the guys to know I'm there for him."

"Are you?" Mary asked.

"I am. I love him. I've never, erm, I've never needed or wanted an audience."

"Crazy knows what he's doing. He'll protect you throughout it all. No one will touch you, and tomorrow, it will be like it never happened," Holly said, slapping Zoe's hand away.

The oven pinged, letting Leanna know it was time to remove the lasagna from the oven.

She placed it on a cooling tray. It would be too damn hot to eat now. Moving to the frosting, she grabbed a bag, and started piping frosting onto each cake. Tasting a little of the cream cheese frosting onto her finger, she moaned. It tasted really good, better than good.

When all the work was done, they carried the food out to the table. She had put the lasagna down on the table, and taken a step away, and now the men were around it. Holly and Mary burst out laughing, and Leanna's eyes widened.

"I told you they loved that lasagna," Crazy said, pulling her back against him. He held onto her tightly, and she leaned back, resting her head on his shoulder.

"I don't think there will be enough for you."

"I've got the cook. You can make some for me tomorrow."

Leanna chuckled, and watched as the lasagna was gone within minutes. She left Crazy's arms to grab a couple of burgers from Duke.

Russ and Sheila were taking care of all of the kids for the party. They knew tonight was going to be the night that Crazy claimed her in front of the club. Her nerves were wound so tight, but she forced herself to keep calm, and not to run screaming. It was hard to do with everyone around.

Crazy stayed by her side, holding her close. His fingers teased her body by stroking her neck, or touching her breasts. He did it in such a way that no one saw, and she was thankful. With their gazes away from her, she tried to think about something else.

"Relax, Leanna. No one is going to pounce on you. This is what I want, and I promise you, I will protect you."

Her body was in his hands, and she did trust him. She trusted him with her whole heart and soul. Glancing down at the ring that decorated her finger, her resolve was made up. She wasn't going to run away from him. This was what he needed for the club to know she belonged to him, and she had his back.

You can do this for your man.

Other old ladies had done this before, and it was her turn.

She had the strength to do what needed to be done.
****

The night wore on, and when darkness fell, the music was turned up, and Crazy took her hand. He'd seen Duke nod in his direction, and it was time for a handful of the brothers to gather within the club.

Leanna didn't try to stop him from taking her into the clubhouse. Landon closed the door behind him, keeping guard so no one entered. The claiming of an old lady was a private affair, and didn't require any of the club whores present. This was about the member and his woman. Tonight, it was about him and Leanna. No one else. Mary and Holly were there. Raoul and Zoe had gone to his room. Daisy, Knuckles, Pie, and Smash were all there, along with a couple of other brothers.

He took her into the clubroom, and some soft music had been played. No one gave them any notice as he took her toward the pool table.

"I love you, Leanna."

"I love you, too." Her gaze darted around the room, and he turned to see they were being watched. He'd done some watching himself, and their gazes didn't bother him.

"Look into their eyes, Leanna. They're not judging you. They're waiting to see if you'll reject me."

"I'm not going to reject you."

He fingered the straps of her dress, and tugged

them down her arms until her full breasts fell free. Crazy moaned at the sight, and took one hard bud into his mouth, sucking the tip. Moving to the next one, he gave it the same kind of attention. Leanna sank her fingers into his hair, and he groaned at the bite of pain from her fingers.

"Look at them, Leanna. They're accepting you as my woman. No one else is ever going to touch you." He pulled away, and removed his leather cut, placing it on her. "See, you belong to me. You're my property, my woman, and I'm going to love you for the rest of my life."

"Make me your woman in the eyes of the club, Crazy."

He lifted her up onto the table, and slid his hands underneath her dress. She wriggled her hips as he removed her panties, pocketing the fabric. Unbuckling his belt, he released his zipper, and pulled out his cock.

They hadn't worn a condom the last couple of times, and he wasn't about to start now. He wanted her pregnant, and had even started reading books ready for when she was pregnant. He'd not taken the time with Suz, as he hadn't believed in the beginning that Strawberry was his.

With Leanna, he was determined to do everything right.

"I need you, Crazy."

Sinking his fingers into her hair, he slammed his lips down on hers, plunging his tongue into her mouth, and kissing her deeply. He couldn't believe the way he felt about her. It was pure love, need, and everything in between. Leanna made him a better person, and he would do everything to show her how much he loved her.

Finding her pussy, he pushed the tip of his cock inside her. For the last three weeks he'd fucked her every chance he got, and she was still incredibly tight, squeezing him.

"I love you," he said, slamming all the way inside her.

She cried out, and released her so that she could lie back on the pool table, wrapping her legs around his waist. He pulled out of her, watching his slick cock appear. Without waiting a moment, he slammed back inside, going so deep that it took both of their breath away. Crazy stared around and saw the brothers watching him claim his woman, his real woman. He'd never done this for Suz, and with their gazes on him, he knew Leanna had won their trust and loyalty.

No matter what happened, she would be protected, and loved by the club.

Fucking her hard, he stroked her clit, and as she came apart, he found his own release, growling out his words of love and acceptance.

Leanna sat up, winding her hands around his neck, and pressing kisses to his neck.

"I love you."

"Look at them, Leanna."

She looked over his shoulder.

"Do you see it?"

"They're not judging me."

"You took Crazy as your man. You came out of your comfort zone. You're one of us, Leanna," Duke said.

Picking his woman up, he waved at his men, and Leanna giggled as he carried her upstairs.

"You're going to hurt yourself."

"No, I'm not. I'm not done with you yet."

Kicking his door closed, he dropped her to the bed, and pulled out of her pussy. "Take the dress off." She went to remove his jacket, and he stopped her. "No, I want you to keep the jacket on."

She removed her dress and underwear.

Taking his own clothes off, he sat on the bed. "Turn for me."

She gave him a twirl in the leather jacket. "You're all mine now, and I'm not letting you go."

"You promise?"

"I need you, Leanna. You call to me."

Leanna moved to him, kneeling over either side of his legs. "You promised me something." She took his hand, and placed it on her ass. "And now I'm ready for it."

"You want me to fuck that pretty ass?"

"Yes. I do."

"Get on your knees."

Tonight was going to be the first night of many, and Crazy couldn't wait to live the rest of his life. Until Leanna opened her heart to him, he'd only been surviving, and now he was finally living.
****

"Tomorrow is mine and Beth's last day," Maria said.

Daisy sat up, turning to the raven haired woman who had driven him crazy. "She got over whatever she needed to?"

"I don't know. The summer is over, and it's back to the real world." Her arms were folded over her chest. She looked restrained, closed off, and unattainable.

"The real world? Where people lie, live a false life to show the world how perfect they are."

"Not everyone is like that."

"You'll fit right in."

Maria cursed. "I'm sick of this. You have pushed and pushed all summer, trying to prove you're something. I've seen you with the club whores. Does it feel good to screw women who don't care about you? Who don't give a shit?"

"Yeah, it does. They don't run from me."

"You're wrong about me, and you can't even see what's right in front of you."

Daisy frowned, and panicked as she turned to leave his room. Jumping off the bed, he rushed toward her, grabbing her arm.

"What the hell are you talking about?"

"You think I can't handle you, but you're wrong. You don't know anything about what I want, what I need."

"Then tell me."

Maria growled. "I want to be owned, cherished, loved, and I want to trust someone so that I can give my body, heart, and mind to. I've seen it happen. I want it."

Daisy panted. "You want college."

"No. I know what I want, and I can't have it. I'm not allowed to. I have to be independent, and want to make a name for myself. I'm doing everything everyone wants for me, and I'm not getting a thing that I want."

Tears filled her eyes and spilled over.

His heart was pounding. "Then stay."

"What?"

"Stay, and let's see where this will go."

"You don't mean that."

"I do. Stay at the club, be mine."

"Beth?"

"She doesn't want to leave. She told me that last night. I'll call our parents, and you can do college online. Stay."

"And?"

"And we'll see if you can really handle me being in charge completely."

Epilogue

One month later

Crazy paced outside of the bathroom, and Strawberry sat reading a book she'd been learning at school.

"You're wearing out Mom's carpet."

He stopped pacing outside of the bathroom, and took a seat next to his little girl. Within two days of being at school Strawberry had started calling Leanna "Mom", and he'd seen the emotion in his woman.

"You could be having a baby brother or sister."

"I know. I'll be a big girl."

He chuckled. "I know you would."

Today, Duke had given him the news that Suz had been taken care of. His ex had been sentenced to ten years for attempted murder. Crazy was happy that his family no longer had to worry about Suz coming back to hurt them. There had been a contact in the women's prison, who'd taken pleasure in ending Suz. When the chance for parole came up, the club was going to see to it that she was released.

Crazy heard the toilet flushing, and he stood when the door opened. Leanna held a white stick in her hand.

"It's positive."

He was so damn happy, he released a triumphant scream. "We're pregnant. You hear that, dumpling? We're going to have another little you running around."

Strawberry jumped up, and they all started laughing and dancing. He couldn't contain his excitement. Putting a call through to Duke, he let him hear the good news.

"Congratulations," Duke and Holly said, shouting down the line.

Next, he called the club, and everyone else he knew.

Shouting, cheering, he tugged Leanna into his arms. "We're going to have a baby."

"We're going to have a baby."

"I love you," he said.

"And I love you."

Later that night, after dinner was served, and Strawberry was put to bed, he sat in the bath with Leanna in his arms.

"Are you really happy about having another baby?" she asked.

He tugged some hair off her neck, and pressed a kiss to her neck. "Words can't even begin to describe how happy I am. Didn't you recognize my happiness before?"

She chuckled. "I did."

Running his hands down the front of her body, he placed his palm over her rounded stomach.

"My kid is in there. The baby we made together. Believe me, Leanna, I'm so damn happy. You make me happy."

"I know what you mean. I think I'm going to wake up, and be back at my apartment, and all of this was going to have been a dream."

"This is no dream. I loved you from the first moment I saw you, and I pushed the need down. I couldn't have you because I was married to a woman I couldn't stand. I hated Suz, and whenever I was around you, I hated her even more. She stopped me from having you."

Leanne leaned back, and kissed his neck.

"You've got me now."

"I know. This baby is going to be the first of many."

She groaned. "I'm kind of scared. Holly showed me some of the books that have, erm, really clear images."

He chuckled. "I'll be by your side for our first baby, second, third, fourth."

"How many kids do you want?"

"Enough that you can't leave me."

He turned her around and found her warm heat. Sliding his dick deep inside her pussy, they both moaned together. "The moment I took you without a condom, I knew I wasn't ever going to fuck you with one. I want you, Leanna, all the time. You're the love of my life."

"You're mine."

Crazy made love to her deep into the night, and every night after that. When it was time for her to give birth, he was true to his word. He stayed by her side, seeing his son into the world, and it just made him fall even deeper.

Falling in love was real, and so was having a happy ending. He'd found his.

The End

www.samcrescent.com

NEED

EVERNIGHT PUBLISHING ®

www.evernightpublishing.com